Ky

Richard Wayne Bobholz

AuthorHouse™
1663 Liberty Drive
Bloomington, IN 47403
www.authorhouse.com
Phone: 1-800-839-8640

First published by AuthorHouse 02/22/2011

ISBN: 978-1-4567-3805-1 (e)
ISBN: 978-1-4567-3806-8 (hc)
ISBN: 978-1-4567-3807-5 (sc)

Library of Congress Control Number: 2011901592

Printed in the United States of America

This book is printed on acid-free paper.

Prologue

After a series of destructive and deadly wars, a treaty was signed by all nations of the Earth to cease the advancement in offensive weapons and the full disclosure of defensive weapons. However, more arrogant countries, such as the United States, Russia and China, felt as though they were not obligated by this treaty and continued their research. Using the United States as an example, all the countries of Earth turned against the United States in a very short war, leaving it without defense and government completely turning the nation into a wasteland controlled by gangs and violence.

During this brief war, many countries used technology not before seen by the other nations, proving they too, broke the treaty. Another vast and devastating war broke out. Three countries remained neutral: Morocco, Algeria, and Japan.

Morocco and Algeria were far too weak to fight because of a border conflict they fought against each other, and Japan, the only country to obey the treaty, felt they had no part in this war.

After a long war, with most countries either destroyed completely or near destruction, soldiers, not knowing who to be loyal to, started attacking everything. Generals turned on allies, soldiers joined whatever army could feed them, and weapons became a currency. One group of desperate soldiers launched a missile in the wrong direction. It hit the market center of a city in Japan. Japan, outraged, declared they were going to wage war against all warring countries of the earth, since they could not determine who launched the missile. In only two weeks, Japan was victorious, completely tearing apart the already war-ravished Earth.

Japan had no intention of keeping what they conquered, or helping rebuild it, so Morocco, the strongest remaining country, held a conference to determine what would be done to rebuild. It was agreed upon that Morocco would offer loans and material for a hefty one-hundred year-long tax on the countries. Japan, fed-up and foreseeing trouble, left the conference and returned to their island.

Using technology they salvaged from the conquered countries, they developed a massive defense and later a machine that could hide their island from all forms of detection. They wanted no part of this new Earth.

After fifty years of peace and rebuilding, a blunder by Algeria's leader, Sil Marxiq, gave Morocco an open door to conquer Earth. They engulfed the opportunity. Many countries gave up willingly to Morocco's unification ideals, but a few had to be conquered by force. Most were easily dispatched, but some like India, China, and Russia were stubborn in their resistance.

One night, Crotonee, leader of Morocco, finally managed to conquer India, China, and Russia in a sudden, well-organized, attack on all three at the same time.

Introduction

Young boys are filled with thoughts of grandeur. Slowly as boys grow older, they lose this eternal hopefulness that the future brings wondrous things. It is only in those boys who do not lose this hope that find the grandeur they hope for.

Ky Bantoria was one of these young boys. At twelve years of age, his mind raced with plans for the future. With few friends and less in stature, Ky was left only to imagine. He was, by no means, a fit young child. Things in India were hard due to the constant war waging around them. Clothing was hard to come by, so Ky wore whatever he could find. Today, he wore a stretched out tan shirt that extended just past his cutoff jean shorts. Only when Ky lifted his arms could his shorts be seen ending well above his knees.

"Hey, Guys," panted Ky, as he caught up with his friends, "wait up!"

He wasn't dumb. His intelligence was above most people, but he wasn't a genius either. Despite his above average intelligence, school was never his strong point, so most people thought he was lacking in brains. The truth was, he was lazy, a day-dreamer by day and a dreamer by night, always seeing himself as something great, something important. Never could his dreams amount to what he really felt his potential to be. In his dreams, he was a character completely unlike him in real life. He went by the name of Kyriac in his dreams. Kyriac was strong, confident, handsome and charismatic. These traits embodied the perfect person in Ky's mind because he had none of them in real life.

"Hey, Ky, what's happening?" said Stephera, Ky's best friend, and an egotistical twelve-year-old.

His brown, messy, hair stopped bobbing up and down when he reached his friends, but it wouldn't stay out of his eyes. A haircut was hard to come by for him, as there were no professionals to do it, and his mother was no artist. So, he let it grow until it became too long to cope with. This point wasn't near that stage. Right now, though, his hair was at the annoying point in between being short and being long where it was the perfect length to jab Ky's eyes when it up and decided to move, which happened to be nearly every five minutes. As irritating as it was, Ky tolerated it because he knew this stage only lasted a few days.

"Did you hear?" asked Ky. "On the news yesterday night, they said that the old, run-down, abandoned building downtown was scheduled to be demolished."

His shoes were nothing to brag about either with holes revealing his big toe, not even covered by a proper sock, though it was obvious he was wearing socks with the loose fabric tiredly climbing up his leg reaching about halfway to his knee before its strength wore off and it drooped back downward in a mushroom shaped fashion. One of the socks had more strength left in it than the other, so it stayed slightly higher up Ky's leg as if to show dominance over the other leg. The heels of the soles of Ky's shoes were worn down past the rubber because of the way he walked always rolling with the outside of his heel hitting first.

"Which one?" remarked Steve, one of the other boys. "This city is about to wage a war against the empire, all of our buildings are abandoned."

With a small gap in his front teeth and an almost noticeable crooked tooth on his right side, Ky always refrained from smiling, even the slightest bit. He noticed these defects far more than anyone else, though he didn't realize that his smile, regardless of its faults, was a trait special to him. The crooked tooth bothered him so much that every day he pressed against it to try to straighten it out, and over the years, it appeared to be straightening slightly.

"This is the one that had the twenty dead workers in it, so they shut it down," responded Ky.

The most noticeable feature found on this shy kid was his eyes. Occasionally, his eyes would be blue, whereas most of the time, his eyes remained a muted sea green. Ky didn't know what caused his eyes to change colors so frequently, whether it was his emotions or changed based on time of the year or the weather. His favorite color was his green eyes, but his favorite eye color was when his eyes were bright blue.

"Isn't that place haunted?" inquired another boy, Dane.

Today, Ky had with him a meager lunch consisting of only a processed meat sandwich and a bottle of water. His family was poor before the war, as most families were in this day and age, but once the war struck India, goods and services became too expensive for almost all families to buy. Ky was fortunate his family was small so they could afford to provide this lunch of his. Dinners, at his home, weren't much different from this lunch.

"Hey, I dare you to spend the night there, since you think it is haunted and all," dared Ky, "unless you are scared." Ky didn't intend for the conversation to carry any further. He just wanted to look tough.

To say that these other boys were Ky's friends was Ky's point of view. They were, in fact, a group of kids too nice to tell him otherwise. They tolerated his company, even enjoying it on the rare occasion, but he wasn't a friend of theirs. He was never invited to anything with them and was never included in any of their plans.

"No way!" exclaimed the boy.

Stephera was the only one who ever invited Ky, or included him in anyway, but that was just because Stephera was nice.

"Why? Are you scared?"

Ky found himself doing things he would otherwise find ridiculous or obscene just so he could fit in with these other kids. He longed for a sense of friendship so much he would do anything, anything at all for the attention.

"No...Why don't you spend the night there yourself since you're not scared of it?" retorted Dane back at Ky calling Ky's earlier bluff.

Ky felt trapped, so he looked for support from the only one there who ever gave any to him, Stephera.

"Yeah, Ky, why don't you?" asked Stephera, demoralizing Ky's hope to get out of this.

Ky knew he had started this whole idea, and he felt horrible knowing he caused himself to get into this position as he commonly did when he tried to act like one of the other guys.

"Because I dared him first," replied Ky as he glared at Stephera.

Completely desperate and trapped, Ky tried to reason with his eyes to Stephera as though he had some special power over the entire group, as though Stephera were a god of this gathering.

"So, we all dare you," said the boy mockingly.

Ky found himself staring at the holes in his shoes, admiring the way most of the shoe held up except the holes at the ends where his toes showed through, and the realization that his shoelaces were two distinctly different colors.

"Fine," conceded Ky, "for one night and you guys are supplying all the stuff I need."

Ky always found himself being pushed around by the other kids because he was timid and wouldn't stand up for himself, so he would try things like this to make himself appear tougher than he was. He always felt small and insignificant, but he continued to do what the other boys told him to do because he thought they were his friends.

The abandoned building wasn't talked about for the rest of the day. Ky thought that idea had been dropped altogether.

The next day, Friday, some of Ky's friends came up to him and asked if he was doing it tonight. Ky was confused at first, but then he realized they were talking about the abandoned building.

"Oh, of course," mumbled Ky as he gulped air that left the taste of fear knotted in the back of his throat so he could still taste it, but in a spot where he couldn't swallow.

"All of the stuff you will need I have at my house," said Stephera, "Just stop by after school."

It wasn't the idea that the building was haunted that scared Ky. He didn't believe in ghosts. It was the fact that people were mysteriously found dead there. There had to be something weird going on with the building. More than that, though, was the idea of being alone. He had never had to be completely alone, ever, and that idea scared him.

"Yeah, I'll do that."

The school day crawled passed for Ky. He kept thinking about what was going to happen to him that night.

After school, Ky met up with Stephera. Slowly, they walked towards Stephera's house.

"Hey, my mom is making her homemade pasta dish that you always enjoy so much," exclaimed Stephera trying to cheer Ky up.

"I don't really feel like eating right now."

"Well you have to eat, so I recommend you enjoy your last meal," Stephera said with a slight chuckle beneath his breath.

"Oh thanks for putting it that way."

They arrived at Stephera's house. Susan, Stephera's mom, greeted them at the door. She smiled cheerfully at them, but Ky frowned and looked away.

Ky walked over, took the phone off the hook, and asked, "Can I use your phone to call my mom?"

"Yeah, go right ahead," affirmed Susan.

"Hey, mom, um, can I spend the night at Stephera's house?" queried Ky with the hopes that she would say no.

"Oh sure!" exclaimed Ky's overzealous mother, Jane, loud enough for Stephera to hear.

"Dinner's ready!" shouted Susan from the dining room.

"Thanks," murmured Ky as he hung up the phone and inched into the dining room and over towards the table.

Ky didn't eat much during that meal. For him, this was the end of the world. He was afraid of that building and what the building represented to him.

Dinner ended. It was time for Ky to go to the abandoned building. In silence, Ky gathered a flashlight, sleeping bag, snacks, and pillow that Stephera had supplied him.

Ky and Stephera walked the half-mile journey to the abandoned building. To Ky, the ten minute walk felt like two hours. Walking silently, Ky tried to create some excuse why he would be unable to stay at the building, but he created none.

The building was at one point a three story, but now stood only two. With the ongoing war, the city could not allocate resources towards keeping some buildings. This region of town suffered because of it. There were hardly any intact buildings within a couple of blocks. However this one was the worst. Though the building still stood two stories tall, the second floor was inaccessible because there was no floor there. The second floor had fallen into the first floor.

Outside the building Stephera said, "Don't worry, nothing's going to happen to you. You can back out, if you're a chicken."

"Yeah, right," Ky said as he walked into the building all alone, still attempting to act brave in front of Stephera.

As soon as Ky entered the building, he could smell the rotting and the musty air.

It was a bright and clear afternoon, but in that building it was dark, damp, and cold. To Ky it felt like walking through a graveyard at night with someone stalking him. He comforted himself by mumbling, "What kind of an idiot would be in here?"

After looking around for a little bit, his hyperactive imagination took over him to the point that he thought someone was there with him trying to kill him. In a panic, Ky became tired and dizzy so he sat down.

He woke up, a few hours later, to the sound of voices and a click. It was much darker than when he had arrived. Walking over to where he heard the noises, he turned on his flashlight and curiously explored the area. After about a half hour of searching, he stumbled upon a small handle. He pulled on it and the wall gave way to reveal a long, bright, and completely non-expected hallway.

The bright light flooding the area blinded Ky for a few seconds. After regaining his vision, he saw a long hallway about six feet wide with doors and corridors on both sides. His imagination took hold once more. In a daze he dropped the flashlight, leaving his sleeping bag and miscellaneous supplies behind, Ky curiously headed down the hallway. He was no further than fifty feet into it when he heard voices again. He darted into the nearest room. Fortunately, it was unoccupied. The room stored enough food to feed the entire city for at least a month he thought. He heard the people stop right outside the door. One of them entered. Ky ducked behind a shelf. A man turned on the lights. Ky could now see the man clearly. He was wearing a white lab coat, which caused Ky's curiosity to swell once more. He knew he should probably leave the complex for the sake of his life, but he was too curious for his own good. As soon as the man left, Ky got up, went to the door, and pressed his ear up to it to find out if anyone was near. It sounded clear, so Ky left the pantry.

He peered up and down the hallway. Nobody was in sight. Ky walked fast down the hall. He could see the end. There was a small opening with a larger, elaborate, doorway. Ky had a strange feeling that all of his questions would be answered inside that door. He had almost reached the door when two men, with automatic machine guns, stepped out from a corridor. Ky stopped dead in his tracks, hoping they wouldn't see him, but it was useless for a kid wearing a red shirt in a white hallway.

"Hey! What are you doing in here?" shouted one of the soldiers.

"Come with us," demanded the other.

Without a choice, Ky followed, wondering what his fate may be. They brought him to a nice cedar paneled room with various books on several wooden bookshelves and set him down in a comfortable velvet padded chair. This room appeared to be an office of someone important. The nameplate on the desk read: "Ritwo." Ky assumed Ritwo felt he was too important to be referred by a last name, or perhaps Ritwo was his last name and he didn't go by his first.

"Ritwo, we got an intruder," announced one of the soldiers.

"Really?" inquired Ritwo from a back room.

"Tis a small boy," smirked the other soldier.

Ritwo's head popped out from the back room as he said, "What!?! A boy found his way in here?"

"Seems that way, sir"

"Guards you are dismissed," barked Ritwo.

"Yes, Sir!" the two soldiers barked in response.

"Hello, my name is Ritwo. By what shall I address you?" asked Ritwo in a calm tone after the guards had left.

There was a long pause before Ky decided to answer, "you can call me Ky."

"Well, Ky," started Ritwo. "Are you for or against the unification?"

Being caught off guard, he decided to answer truthfully. "I'm against it, sir."

"Good boy," Ritwo said cheerfully.

A sigh of relief came out of Ky. Ritwo thought for a short moment then said, "I am the leader of a technology center for the rebellion. My latest project could turn the course of this war in our favor. Everything is going as planned right now, and we need nothing that could possibly cause us error right now. We are on a strict deadline. Understand?" There was a short pause and then Ritwo added, "I will lead you out of here, and it is very important that you tell absolutely no one about this. It is very important for you, me, and our country."

Ky proudly said, "You can count on me."

"Good."

Ritwo led Ky to the door where he had entered. As they got near, red lights began flashing and a soldier ran up to them and said, "Ritwo, we have a problem in the lab. We need you there immediately."

"Ky, there's the exit, go! I must leave now," exclaimed Ritwo as he ran towards down the hall.

Ky took two steps toward the exit when his curiosity got the best of him once more. He turned around and proceeded to the large doors he'd seen earlier. This time the guards didn't find him. The door was wide open and everyone was too busy to notice. Ky snuck under a silver instrument cart and looked around the lab.

In the center of the lab stood a large glass tube filled with water and what appeared to be a body floating in the middle. Next to the tube was a metal body and a large array of equipment that Ky disregarded as simply tools. In the back of the lab, sat a piece of equipment that Ky recognized. He had done a school project on it once. It was called an Electro-Magnetic Crystalline Pulse-Wave Generator. It creates a very large, controlled stream of energy, and its primary advantage was how much energy it created for its small size. The generator was no larger than an adult human's heart. A piece of equipment like that costs about two hundred and seventy billion dollars. Ky wondered how they got one of those in a place like this.

Then Ky saw Ritwo as he walked over to the Electro-Magnetic Crystalline Pulse-Wave Generator, or EPG for short, picked it up, and brought it over to the metal body. Ritwo placed the EPG in the chest area that one of the other men had just opened. Then the scientists transferred the metal body into a mold.

At the same time, a few scientists drained the tube in the center of the lab. The body became a glob in the bottom of the tube. Ky blinked and the glass of the tube disappeared from his vision. He assumed it either went into the ceiling or floor. The scientists were using several instruments to move the glob over to the mold. They carefully placed it over the metal body, and then sealed it before they proceeded to separate computer panels.

Ky could no longer see what was going on, so he started scooting the cart closer to the area where the scientists were working. One of the scientists noticed the cart moving and shouted, "Too much gravitational intake. Release power."

A few scientists started adjusting the equipment, but then one of the instruments next to Ky malfunctioned. As Ky was scooting the cart, static electricity built up on the cart and a spark flew from the cart to the console next to Ky damaging some of the hardware. The machine Ky had ruined regulated the output of the crystalline power, so the crystal went into a state of chaos. A wave of crystallized energy shot out from the mold. It looked like glowing Ice, but steaming hot. Ritwo saw it before it reached him and he dove into the air and spun over it and landed on his back. Most of the scientists were cut to shreds, like chunks of glass ripped at their skin, and died instantly, or they held on to their lives long enough to say a last prayer. Ritwo was still alive. As he got up, he whirled around, and he saw Ky in the cart. Ky and Ritwo made eye contact for less than a second, but it was long enough. Ky knew he caused this, and so did Ritwo.

"You!" shouted Ritwo as he bounded across the lab.

Ky immediately lunged out from under the cart and out the door. Filled with adrenaline, he felt like he had ten times as much power as he normally did. Ritwo sprinted after him. Ky, finding a new strength in himself, doubled his speed and headed straight for the exit. Before he could turn the handle, Ky collided with the door and went with the door as it fell to the ground. He slid about 20 yards through the dust and dirt of the abandoned building. In a matter of seconds, Ritwo was right over him and picked him up by his neck with amazing ease. Ky kicked Ritwo in his face, and he immediately dropped Ky and stumbled backwards.

With a sense of urgency, Ky rose and took off down the street. Before he got half a block away from the building, Ritwo tackled him and slammed him into the concrete. Ky took one swing at Ritwo's stomach and nailed it. Gasping for breath, Ritwo, still on top of Ky, threw his fist at Ky's face. Ky moved swiftly and Ritwo punched the concrete. Ky broke free of Ritwo's grasp and ran down the street. He ran straight back to Stephera's house. Ritwo decided he couldn't pursue Ky because he had to clean up his lab and find out what could be salvaged of his work, but someday, he decided, he would track him down. He would never forget his face.

Ky, now back at Stephera's house, was telling a skeptical, yet tolerant, Stephera the entire story. While he explained what had happened, the city's sirens went off, and several explosions happened simultaneously. Stephera looked out the window to see explosions happening all over the city and surrounding areas. The explosions were still far enough away to not cause an immediate threat, but they were coming in quickly.

Stephera's mom tried to get them out of the city, but the roads were packed and traffic was at a standstill. An explosion went off right next to their car, shattering the windows and sending a mangled fiery body of a car with three passengers down a three hundred foot drop landing on only rocks and other cars for comfort. The screams were deafening. It landed with a crash, and a few more cars landed on and around it. The impact caused Ky to hit his head and pass out, but he was miraculously still alive.

Ky awoke a few minutes later lying in the mangled wreck of Stephera's car. He could hear more explosions, but they were further away now. Stephera was hunched over with his neck only partially connected to his back, and his mom had half a steering wheel embedded in her skull. Ky was scratched up badly and had a broken arm and a few broken and bruised ribs. The screams from the fall were the only things he could hear, still fresh in his mind. He began to cry. Instead of trying to hold it back as he usually would do, he just let it flow. As he cried, he made a promise that he would get revenge on all those who kill people. He didn't know how, or even why, but if felt like that was what he had to do.

Eventually, Ky regained his strength and, despite his broken bones, traveled out of the warring area to an island near the cloaked nation of Japan. The same strike that wiped out Ky's town happened all through India and Russia. Eventually it reached China. Even though China was ready for them and put up a long fight, they lost in the end. Japan was the only country not to fall under the empire under guard of their cloak shield. Millions of people traveled to Japan to escape the empire's rule, and Japan warmly welcomed anyone who opposed Crotonee.

Chapter 1

Ritwo, like most powerful people, liked power, and through deception and his vast intelligence of military equipment, Ritwo constantly wrestled for more of it. As the Scientist General of India, he was in a position to his liking, but in one night, his power was stripped from him, first through Ky's destruction of his lab, and second, through the Empire's invasion of India. The weaponry that Ritwo had designed was impressive, but they couldn't hold up to the sheer force the Empire sent in that night.

Though his army was destroyed, his inventions capture, and his plans foiled, Ritwo was neither captured nor discouraged. As a scientist, he entered the ranks for the Empire. Shortly thereafter, he was noticed and employed personally by Crotonee to continue his work. Crotonee had no idea who he was or what he was working on in India, nor could he have known of any ulterior motives. What Crotonee did know was that Ritwo had a good heart and an even better mind. For these, Crotonee employed him. When Crotonee needed a problem solved, he turned to Ritwo. Through time, they had even become friends.

His trust for Ritwo was immense. It was enough that when Crotonee passed on, he had appointed Ritwo as the new Guardian of Earth. Ritwo and the Council were both deeply surprised by this move.

The Council, a group of twelve generals, followed the Guardian's orders directly. The guardian made decisions based upon the Council's advice, and the Council ran parts of the Empire based upon the Guardian's orders. In theory, neither had power without the other. The Guardian did not have a military, so he was dependent upon the Council, and supposedly, the Council members could be replaced by the Guardian. Ritwo's only real power came from the other council members. If enough of them opposed him, he would no longer have that power. Because all the council members were loyal to Crotonee before the unification even started, it was not hard for him to control them. They respected him, but few respected Ritwo. Ritwo's council was split between those who oppose his rule and those who didn't care. He had very few supporters.

It was the third day of Ritwo's reign and several councilmen had publicly disclaimed loyalty to him the day before. On top of that, the guards that protected Crotonee's palace decided to desert leaving Ritwo virtually unprotected.

The Guardian was the only thing that kept the Council from becoming separate factions, but as Ritwo was quickly realizing, they were already separate factions immediately after Crotonee's death.

Only hours after the guards deserted, there was a stern knock on the door of the palace. Ritwo hadn't arranged any meetings yet, and if even he had, there was an office in the Council Building for him to use. Additionally, despite the fact that there were no guards, the palace grounds were hard to get on to. Nerves should have taken over here, but frustration took hold of Ritwo instead. "How am I supposed to protect the planet if I can't protect my own home?" He bolstered, and added challengingly, "let them in!"

Jev, the personal guard and servant to Ritwo, swung the door open. On the other side stood a man, no taller than five and a half feet. A dark shroud covered his entire body except his sickly brown eyes and one scared hand that grasped onto a walking stick. Either this man was dying, or he had been in a horrible fire or explosion.

"What do you want?" Jev asked.

The man's eyes moved from Jev to Ritwo in the background. "You," he growled in a voice that didn't sound at all sick. "I represent a member of the Council who kindly requests that you step down. My name is Extonic Jarod, and I will be replacing you."

"That's not going to happen," laughed Ritwo.

"Rest assured, it will," Extonic calmly explained. "I am glad you're stubborn though. I wouldn't want any of this to end peacefully. It's a new order, and the weak cannot stand to rule this Earth."

As Extonic took a step forward, Jev put his hand out as if to ask him to stay where he was. In one swift motion, Extonic parried Jev's arm with his stick, punched him in the stomach, and while he was hunched over, kicked him in the side of the face, tossing him to the side.

"You know nothing of the grave need of the world," Extonic continued, unabated by his feat. "There are people dying of starvation, gangs that run parts of this world, and murderous villains running rampant through our cities. In three days, you've managed to do nothing. In the world we live in, we cannot spare three days."

From watching Jev tossed aside so easily, Ritwo was afraid. He barely heard any of the words Extonic spoke. He wore an electronic shield that protected him from small massed objects like bullets, but he didn't expect someone to kill him with martial arts. He always thought that fighting with fists was a thing of ancient history, relying heavily on his science. Now, the fists of one man were going to be his downfall.

Extonic chuckled as Ritwo tried to form what he thought was a defensive stance. "Never been in a fight before, have you?" he asked.

Ritwo drew his gun and shot Extonic right in the chest, but the bullet was stopped just before it reached him. No doubt he had the same type of shield as Ritwo had. In the middle of Extonic's now full-bellied laugh, Jev leaped to his feet and took a mighty swing at Extonic's head. Somehow aware of the oncoming attack, Extonic leaned back, allowing the punch and part of Jev's body to cross over top of him. Once Jev's torso crossed over Extonic's body, Extonic pushed off with his feet into a back handspring, ensuring to kick Jev in the chest and send him flying out the door as he performed his acrobatics.

Jev, in pain, looked up to see four burly soldiers right before they hit him with something that made him black out.

With his bodyguard gone, and Ritwo having no concept of how to fight, he decided to come out swinging. He ran at Extonic. Extonic dodged his first punch and responded with a punch to the stomach. Ritwo was tough and ignored the pain. He swung again. This time, Extonic grabbed his arm and pulled on it as he punched Ritwo three times in the face as hard as he could. The first hit knocked Ritwo out, but the three hits happened so fast, Extonic had finished them before realizing Ritwo was unconscious and falling to the ground.

Chapter 2

Meanwhile, on an isolated island near Japan, Ky was working on his individual training. He was now seventeen and even stronger than he had ever imagined.

It was midday and Ky was tired and hungry, so he grabbed his favorite stick and started out on a hunt. After an hour, he spotted a pig in a clearing. Being careful not to scare the pig, he quietly approached, pounced on the pig, and broke its neck. The pig died instantly. He carried it back to his camp with ease. The pig weighed half as much as Ky, but that was nothing for him after these five years.

Ky wasn't the only one to start out on this island. Over a dozen people ended up here, but throughout the five years, all of them had disappeared. Some of them created rafts to attempt to travel back to the mainland, others died of diseases or accidents that couldn't be healed with no medical aid, and a couple simply disappeared with no warning. Originally, Ky had to depend on the others for help hunting and surviving. He couldn't do much on his own when he was twelve, but within a year, he was the only hunter, bringing in enough food for everyone to eat. Others would spend their time gardening, fixing their houses, creating tools or building their own boats to get off the island.

Despite having company on this island for the first few years, the stay was gloomy and sad. Every person on the island had lost someone or left someone behind. No one could comfort the others because no one was without great loss. The only words spoke were when words were needed. They all knew that each had loss, but no one wanted to bring up the dark memories of those tragedies.

After two years on the island, nearly everyone was gone. Only Ky and Nicholas were left, but Nicholas left one night to try to find his family back on the mainland. Ky watched him leave; staying on the island because he knew the search was useless. He knew that not only would he never reach the mainland on a makeshift raft, but he wouldn't be able to find his family and friends because they were all dead. He knew Nicholas was going to his death in the middle of the ocean, but he couldn't say anything because Nicholas knew it too and was leaving like a dog to die alone. Ky was determined to wait out his days on this lonely island all by himself, and for nearly three years, he did so, all by himself, day after day, surviving by his lonesome.

Ky now hunted for himself, maintained the gardens created by the other occupants, and did all the building and crafting himself. The hunting was easy because there were several types of pigs and other small herbivores found on this island with seemingly no predators, but everything was lonely.

Ky sat down in the dirt, on just another day, legs crossed, with the pig directly in front of him. He placed one hand under the pig, and the other, on top of it. Then, he concentrated on creating heat in his hands. Shortly after he started, a mirage of heat radiated from his hands. Ky focused his energy to his hands to the point that they get so hot that they cook things, and if he concentrated really deeply, he could make the heat pass between his hands, cooking the pig from the inside.

He figured out this skill on a cold rainy night when he held onto one girl as he tried to warm her to save her life from hypothermia. Feeling so helpless with this girl's life draining in his arms, a warm glow started to radiate from his entire body. He didn't know what was going on, but with this girl's life, possibly the life of the only friend he had on the island, literally in his arms, he searched for whatever was causing this warmth. He found a strange feeling within him and caused it to increase. His heart rate flared, his breathing increased rapidly and his veins swelled. He could feel the energy running through his entire body. Ky continued to produce this strange heat throughout that rainy night keeping this girl alive while she slept so peacefully. When the morning came, Ky had exhausted himself, but the rain stopped and the sun came out, and even more importantly, the girl's fever had dropped.

The girl didn't remember what Ky had done, but she knew he did something. Before she left the island in search of peace with those she left behind, she thanked Ky with a smile and the words, "thank you." In her days on the island, those were the only words she spoke. A few weeks after she left, her body washed up on the island's shore. Ky shed his last tears before he buried her. He didn't know her name, but he created a tombstone that read, "Tragedy can lead to the fall of even the most beautiful. Such beauty masked with such sadness." Ky had loved this girl, but he didn't know it until she was gone. For the next three and a half years, he visited her grave every week to clear it of weeds and leave her fresh flowers he found throughout the island. "I wish I could've saved you a second time," he'd always apologize to her. "I'm so sorry."

Strangely, Ky's hands came to no harm when he produced this heat. Nearly twenty minutes after starting, the pig was cooked enough to be eaten. He grabbed his sharpened stick and cut a piece off of the roasted pig, continuing to eat until he was nearly full.

Right before he finished his meal, he heard a ship in the distance. He shoved the last piece of meat in his mouth and scaled up a tree. From the tree, Ky could make out the ship. He couldn't see any logo, so he assumed it wasn't an Empire ship. After he watched the ship for a short while, he realized it was heading straight for him, as if it had some sort of Ky radar.

Ky jumped off the tree, landed in his canoe type boat, and started paddling straight for the ship, getting faster and faster on a direct course, as though he were playing chicken with a ship five thousand times larger than his.

Ky's boat rammed into the ship shooting wooden splinters onto the hull. At that moment, Ky jumped aboard. Everyone onboard looked over to where Ky had just landed. They all stared at him for a while just as they would if he had just done something truly amazing. Ky, on the other hand, thought nothing of his actions.

No one could think of what to say, but finally, one spoke. "Hello, my name is Ice," said one of the people on the boat after his short bit of starring. Then he reached out his hand and asked, "What is your name?"

"Ky," he replied as he shook Ice's hand finding talking a strange, but enjoyable feeling. "Is this a military ship?"

"Well, sort of," responded Ice. "This is a private militia, my army."

"This is your army?" inquired Ky.

"Yes, it is," boasted Ice. "Here let me introduce you to them. This is Aqua. He is my primary apprentice. This over here is Inferno. And finally there is Hydra. Hydra is a purebred Archon." As he was introducing them, he gestured towards the person he was speaking of.

In the year 2252, a group of scientists and very curious civilians were part of an experiment known as the Archon project. The goal of the Archon project was to create a super human being. The idea behind this was to remove a human's lungs to make room for plant-like systems to store and produce energy. The host's skin was also transplanted with plant cells that, using photosynthesis, create energy and oxygen for the body's use. After countless trials, in the year 2296, one host survived; his body was 120% the efficiency of an average human being. This sparked interest among many thousands of people who sought the dream of becoming a super-human.

For the next ten years, after the first host, 12,000 people joined project Archon. Fearing the stronger and more versatile Archon, human governments around the world banned the transformation to Archon since, by this point, their bodies were 560% that of a normal human body.

In the year 2311, a widespread dislike and persecution of all Archons began. Many were killed, and they quickly realized they had to flee to a remote area, but the only area left to flee was the ocean, so they did. The advantage of being part plant was their ability to survive in salt water absorbing nutrients quite well. They found that their bodies became even stronger in the ocean. Some even reached 1620% efficiency.

Still people tried to kill them. In many cases people hunted them for sport. By the year 2319, there was only one Archon city, hidden from all humans. This city was commonly referred to as Atlantis, though its real name was Pacticia. Slowly, the population died. Most Archons could not reproduce Archon children since the operations, in most cases, were not genetically altering their bodies, and those that could reproduce were too few that the population would eventually die out of inbreeding.

"Nice to meet you all, but none of that means anything to me," explained Ky. "I've been on that island since the empire invaded my town. Thanks for picking me up. Now, where can you drop me off?"

"You've been on an island for over five years then? That's an incredible amount of time. Are there others?" asked Aqua.

"No, there were, but they're all gone now, either dead or gone in search of the mainland," explained Ky with a sad expression. "Why are you here?"

"We are looking for the notorious Dariah and Beronith. They are the only known mix breed between human and Archon, and they are extremely strong and feared. The two of them were born with a prophecy on their head. Nobody outside the temple knows of the prophecy, other than us. I want them in my army to help fight the empire," explained Ice, and after a short while included, "you seem to be in fairly good shape. Have you ever considered joining the military?"

"When I was younger, I did," explained Ky, "but I just want to get back at the Empire. I don't think a small army is the best way to do that." Ky hadn't decided exactly what he was going to do once he got off the island, so he was making it up as he went at this point. "I want to kill Crotonee," he continued.

"What timing," laughed Ice. "Crotonee died four days ago."

All of a sudden, Ky felt angry. All his anger was directed at Crotonee, so it was easy to control. Now, he had nothing to be angry at. With his anger rising, so did his body heat. There was a chilly breeze on the boat, so when that breeze turned to heat coming from Ky, everyone noticed immediately.

"What is that?" exclaimed Aqua. His voice made Ky snap back to the present moment, and he calmed the storm within him. "Seriously," Aqua continued, "what was that?" Ky then took a few minutes and explained the story of the cold rainy night.

"I'll strike up a deal with you," offered Ice. "I'll train you in the martial arts if you join my army, and teach me how to focus my energy like that."

"It sounds like a good deal, except I'm not interested in being part of any army. I don't exactly have anywhere to go, so I'll go with you guys for a while, though," offered Ky. "Sound good?"

"That sounds like a good plan," said Ice, knowing he wasn't going to get any more out of him.

"Sir, we are almost to the destination," chimed the robotic captain of the vessel. "Your armors have been prepared, and Ky, I have prepared armor for your temporary usage."

"Suit up men!" barked Ice. "We don't know what is waiting for us, or who."

Ice, Aqua, Inferno, and Hydra went to the suiting room while Ky followed them. Ky had no troubles putting on his armor. It was a lightweight, fiber-optic camouflage, full plate armor with gloves, boots, helm, chest plates, and leg plates. There was no part of the body left uncovered.

"Ky, these armors are special. They reflect small firearms, up to three pound shells, and they absorb lasers," explained Ice. "but you need to watch out for blades and other melee weapons. Impacts hurt. That means even though bullets won't pierce the armor, they might bruise you, but probably not because of the plating. I'll go into more detail later, if you'd like."

"Well, if this armor is as good as you say it is, I'll have no problems," replied Ky.

"Hey," started Inferno to Ky. "If we face someone here, they'll be wearing this armor too, not nearly the same make, but firearms and such won't hurt them either, and they'll know it. You've got a knife on your armor if you need it. Any enemy will also probably have some sort of close range melee weapon so be careful."

"Okay," Ky acknowledged.

"We probably won't see anyone though," included Aqua. "Most people avoid these kids because they look damn scary. So, relax, but not too much."

The ship set anchor quite a distance away from the coast. It did this for two reasons. One was because it couldn't go much further. The other reason was more important. It was so that it wouldn't be spotted by any opposition they might meet. Ice always takes precautions such as this to ensure the safety of his men.

As the ship set anchor, Ky looked curiously towards the shore and asked, "Do we have to swim from here?"

He wasn't asking anyone in particular, but everyone heard him. Most of them laughed, but Ice walked up to him and told him that they would take a raft ashore. Ky was feeling a bit tired and didn't want to exert the effort to swim to shore. Also, he had been on an island for five years all by himself isolated from technology. Considering these things, Ky did not understand why his question was laughed at. It was just a simple question that he mumbled to himself. Unfortunately everyone heard his question and did find it amusing.

Aqua, Hydra, Inferno, and Ky, fully suited up, loaded into the raft. They had a mission briefing just moments before. On the raft ride to the island, the warriors showed Ky how to use his armor. When they arrived, the four of them climbed out of the raft and scouted down the shore.

"All right, we'll split up in two groups," explained Ice. "Ky and Aqua together, and Inferno and Hydra. If you find anything hit the distress button twice. If you are in distress, keep hitting it until someone shows up, or break it off. Got it? Aqua and Ky go inland. Inferno and Hydra go North. I'll remain here on the ship and watch over you guys. Go!"

Ky and Aqua took off at a rapid pace while Inferno and Hydra took off at a comfortable jog. Conversation between Hydra and Inferno consisted of talk about Ky. Between Ky and Aqua, conversation was hard but eventually did commence.

"I was wondering," commented Ky as they were running, "how strong is Ice? Since he is training someone of your strength, he must be very strong himself."

"He is not that strong, but he's doing pretty well for his age," answered Aqua feeling flattered by Ky's statement.

"He's old? He looks about thirty."

"He used his power and technology to stay young, physically. He is actually over one hundred years old, and still in good health."

"Wow, that's amazing! He's over one hundred right now! Is he going to be the oldest man alive?"

"Most likely," replied Aqua, "his calculations say he'll live to be about one-hundred-ninety-two in an ideal universe."

"*I hope I can live that long,*" thought Ky.

"Hey, do you want to step up the pace a little? I mean, we want to find these guys as soon as we possibly can, right?" suggested Ky.

"What? You can go faster than this?"

"Yeah about three or four times faster." replied Ky.

"I've gotta see this," smirked Aqua, "go for it."

"Okay!" shouted Ky as he flared his energy and took off making Aqua feel as though he were standing still.

Very shortly after Ky had taken off, he came across an opening in which there was a man dressed in silver, holding a spear with a curved blade on one end and a mace on the other, talking to what appeared to be a soldier of his. Ky looked around the opening for a few moments, noticing a troop of about twenty soldiers. He realized what he was supposed to do and he pressed his distress button twice. His attention was drawn to the conversation between the man in silver and the soldier beside him.

"With Ritwo's downfall, we now have a chance to carry out our plans, sir."

"*Ritwo?*" thought Ky, not about to pinpoint why he knew that name.

"Yes, but as soon as we convince Dariah and Beronith to join us, we will have no problems. Make sure our friend Ex knows the plan."

At this point Aqua arrived by Ky.

"Yeah, this is a real problem," explained Aqua as he hit his distress button twice, "This man, the important looking one in silver holding the Safin Spear, is called SilverX. His real name is Sil Marxiq the second. His father ruled Morocco and they both ruled Russia. Now, he is a mafia leader and a member of the Council, and millions of people believe him to be the strongest and most dangerous person in the world."

"I don't care about him, what's our plan?" asked Ky.

"Wait for the others, and then we will all take out the easy targets while avoiding SilverX. The four of us will take SilverX together," Aqua plotted out.

As he finished his plan, Hydra and Inferno arrived at their position. After briefing them, he prepared a multitude of grenades.

"Go!" commanded Aqua as he threw a few dozen grenades randomly about the open field as distractions.

Then Ky lunged for SilverX.

"Not a chance!" cried SilverX as he launched the cable-attached mace end of his Safin Spear at Ky while Ky was soaring towards him.

Ky threw one of his own grenades at SilverX and rolled in midair to avoid the projectile.

SilverX dodged the grenade and saw that his projectile was going to miss, so he retracted it and hurled himself at Ky. He slashed his Safin Spear towards Ky who was still in midair.

Hydra showed up to the rescue by knocking the attack away with a specially crafted Archon Noble Sword. Hydra was then hit hard in the face by SilverX's steel fist, and he crashed into a tree. He showed no sign of movement.

SilverX regained his weapon and turned to finish Ky off. When he turned around, he was greeted by Ky's hand which was glowing with the heat Ky created in it.

SilverX cursed as he got much of his face singed by the heat of Ky's hand as well as injured by the impact of his fast moving fist.

Ky and SilverX went flying opposite directions. By this time, most of the soldiers had passed out, been knocked out, ran away, or where hiding. SilverX was also on the run, still alive, but very angry. He had gotten what he wanted hours ago but decided to stick around to help clean up. Now he had to run out of the area just to preserve his life.

"Ky!" shouted the rest of the warriors. "Where are you?"

Ky was also on the move. Determined not to let SilverX get away, he was darting through trees, going even faster than he had before. To Ky, this was exhilarating like when he hunted. He had never failed in a hunt and didn't intend to fail here.

"*I wonder what else Ky is hiding from me,*" pondered Ice. "*I'll just wait and see.*"

"Hydra, go after Ky. Aqua and Inferno, get back here as fast as you can," Ice commanded to the warriors.

SilverX was getting in his helicopter when Ky arrived in the clearing and shouted, "SilverX! You're not going anywhere!"

"Watch me," boasted SilverX as he pulled out a large cannon type weapon.

Ky's eyes widened so big that they nearly exploded when he saw SilverX pull the trigger and saw the object come out of it. Ky almost exploded, but at the last second, he leaped to his left. Ky, having been startled by this weapon, actually more tripped to his left than he did leap. He tried to run, but his legs got tangled up, and he hit the ground in an act that was far from graceful. The projectile object that SilverX shot at him hit a tree behind Ky and cause Ky to get further injury by being tossed into the air and landing, once again, on the ground.

As Ky lay there, he could hear the helicopter's engine start up. He tried to move, but pain coursed throughout his body. As the engine sped up leaves and debris dashed about Ky burying him. As the helicopter hummed steadily and lift off the ground, Ky gained a sudden burst of energy. He crawled up to his feet, shook off the debris, and watching contently the helicopter that had just started to life off, his feet only hit the ground three times in his bounds over to the helicopter. With the forth bound, he flew aboard.

"Don't you ever die?" asked SilverX as he pulled out a small saber and sliced it at Ky. Ky dodged the slice and kicked SilverX in the chest. SilverX stumbled backwards, but regained himself before he fell out of his helicopter. He countered Ky's attack with a fist. Ky dodged his fist, but SilverX anticipated this and quickly hit him with his other fist. Ky stumbled backwards to the point where his left foot stepped on air. Realizing that his foot didn't hit anything, he jumped with his other foot. Flipping over, he pushed off one of the propeller blades above him and grabbed on to the landing bar on his way back down. SilverX saw what Ky just did, and had to take a few moments to shake off the disbelief.

It was at that point that SilverX decided not to kill him. He motioned for the pilot to lower the helicopter towards the ocean below for when Ky was to fall. Ky hung there motionlessly for only a few seconds, but to him it felt like an incredible amount of time. After those few seconds, Ky swung himself back into the copter to be met by SilverX's fist. Ky went flying out of the helicopter. SilverX, having had his fun, shut the door so no more stray fighters could get in.

Ky had no chance to save himself from that fall. He lay floating atop the water for several minutes. He wasn't dead, but he was disappointed and quite angry. He heard the low purr of Ice's ship approaching him, but he didn't stir from his position. The ship pulled up beside Ky, and Hydra jumped out and swam towards him. He pulled Ky on board and laid him to rest upon a bed in the sleeping quarters.

"Ice, you should've been there and seen what we did. It was incredible!" cheered Aqua.

"I know, I saw," stated Ice and paused for a few seconds, "I saw everything that happened today."

Those were the last words that Ky heard before he fell deep into a coma-like sleep. While Ky was sleeping, Ice explained to his warriors the story of Ricoba, an alien of the Mascien species who could evolve independently. He was the reason Masciens are so powerful now in the universe. Ice then explained that he thought Ky could have the same trait, and that it was now their job to protect him, yet challenge him enough that he is forced to evolve.

Chapter 3

While Ice told his story, a couple thousand miles away, Ritwo and Jev awoke in separate jail cells. The cells were about nine feet by ten feet. The walls appeared to be made of pure steel with an obvious electrical current running through them, and signs indicating so. More threatening than the walls were the bars and beyond.

Ritwo knew, because he designed this cage, that on the bars, the initial electrical current was twice that of the walls and electricity activated chemicals that would kill a person in ten seconds were coating them. Beyond the bars there were three-dozen soldiers. Each soldier was equipped with rocket launchers, high-powered rifles, machine guns and grenades. On the walls outside the cells were at least seventy-two machine gun and grenade turrets. The man holding the controls to Ritwo's sensory collar, however, was the worst.

The collar was linked directly to Ritwo's spinal cord. With the press of a button or the spin of a dial, the controller could inflict any feeling or emotion. This collar was mainly used on slaves or animals when it was first created. Jev was there as added torture; if it came down to it they would shoot him several times until Ritwo cracked.

The medium-built man holding the control wore a white lab coat. He stepped forward towards Ritwo's cell as if to shake hands and introduce himself, then thought better of it. He waited another minute while Ritwo and Jev became more alert, and approached Ritwo's cell once more.

"Well," mocked the man, "it is truly a pleasure to see you again Ritwo. Do you remember me?" Ritwo looked puzzled so the man continued. "I was one of your scientists. The night of the accident, I was there. You thought

I was dead, and in the confusion, my body was left in the building. A few days later, Extonic's men rescued me. You still look confused. Perhaps if I introduce myself you will remember. I am Phil Land, Dr. Land."

The name sounded somewhat familiar to Ritwo, but he was still quite dizzy and tired from being beaten by Extonic and his soldiers. Dr. Land continued. "Nevertheless, welcome to my torture den. It's a nice place, but kind of a harsh name don't you think?"

Ritwo nodded, and he found himself wondering why he nodded. It was, most likely, because of the collar, he concluded.

"And over here, is the legendary Jev. We thought for sure you wouldn't live through that. Of course we thought a lot of things. It's okay Ritwo, that little secret is safe with me," continued Dr. Land, "but the reason we are both here is because I need to return a little bit of information to Extonic. Would you be so kind as to just tell me what I want? I don't want to have to hurt you. You were once my boss, after all, and look, we're both after the same thing." Dr. Land chuckled and went on. "All I need now is the access codes for the Guardian Chamber and the codes for the robotic army. I will also need the recording of you forfeiting your position to Extonic, but I suppose with the first two, a guardian position would no longer be needed."

"I won't talk. This empire should never be in the hands of someone like Extonic," stated Ritwo as he tried to build up his courage. He didn't even try to explain that he had no idea what the robotic army was.

"Oh, but you will. You will talk, eventually. The question is how painful it will be," laughed Dr. Land.

"I will kill myself before I talk!" cried Ritwo.

"You won't, and I'll tell you why. You already know why. I can sense it. But, I will reinforce the information anyway in case you are truly clueless. If you die, the position you hold will be up for grabs by anyone, except the party that killed you. That is true only because you have not created relinquishing papers yet," informed Dr. Land. "I read the entire law book on the Guardian position. It seems Crotonee had his own agenda on how to use the empire. It was unfortunate that he died so soon, but we both know why he died. You found out about his plans, slowly poisoned him, and then befriended him so you may become Guardian. He gave you the position so that you would carry out his plans, but you had your own agenda. Am I on the right track so far?"

Ritwo remained silent. Apparently, Dr. Land had gotten all of the details perfect. Ritwo gazed pathetically at the man, and then turned away.

He suddenly lost all hope of getting out of that cell alive. He tried to look at Jev, but a five-foot thick wall prevented him.

"So, about that information I need," inquired Dr. Land.

"No, I will never..." Ritwo was cut off by Dr. Land pressing a button on the control. Ritwo fell to the floor and was unable to move. All he could manage was breathing.

"Well, I guess we will have to do this the hard way then," mumbled Dr. Land as the bars opened and four soldiers marched in and grabbed Ritwo. They placed him on a table in the corner of the room. Dr. Land pulled the straps tight before releasing Ritwo from being paralyzed. Just as the first shock entered Ritwo, Ky woke up screaming violently in pain.

Ky looked around for a while. It took him a little bit to realize that he was still on the ship. Surprisingly, no one rushed to see what was wrong with him, so he left his cabin and went to the deck. Outside, on the deck, Ky's eyes strained to adjust to the darkness of the night around him. The only light came from the stars in the sky. Except for the slight hum of Ice's ship, it was silent. It was a remarkably low hum considering how fast they were traveling. It had only been a few hours and they were already close to India. What he had experienced earlier, Ky concluded was a dream, but it had seemed so real...

Ky returned to his cabin and lay down to fall asleep, but he couldn't no matter how hard he tried. Each time he would start to doze off, he'd feel the pain and see the images of torture once more. It was now impossible for Ky to sleep, so he didn't. He decided to return to the upper deck and meditate under the open sky.

As he reached the upper deck this time, Ky thought to himself, *"It is too calm and peaceful out here for the world to be as chaotic and hateful as it is."*

With that thought, Ky sat down to meditate. Almost immediately after he started, he was brought back to the place of his dream. He could feel the pain and see the torture, but this time he was the one being tortured. It became impossible to leave the trance. He was stuck in someone else's body, feeling everything he felt and complied with everything he did. He could feel electrical shock waves running through the body he was in and feel the pain in this head he occupied. Ky thought he was going to die even though it wasn't his body being tortured. The pain was unbearable to Ky, who had never experience physical pain such as this.

After a few mere moments of this, Ky was flung from the body and he landed on the ceiling. Dizzy from being thrown from Ritwo's body, Ky noticed everything in the room was moving. He could see many soldiers and the scientist he had seen in his earlier dream. He saw clearly the body of Ritwo lying there, taking all the pain that Ky had just felt, and in that moment while he looked upon Ritwo's helpless body, he pitied this man who once had tried to kill him.

After looking around the room for a while, Ky spotted a door. He went to the door and was about to open it, when his hand went through it. He, then, remembered that he was in a dream and was not actually there. Ky floated through the door to find a hallway on the other side. Still in a daze, Ky drifted down the hallway until he came to another door. This one was many times larger than the last one he had passed through, so he decided it would be a wise idea to pass through this one. On the other side of this door was a courtyard. It was a courtyard of what looked to be a castle. The castle resembled a medieval castle, but with everything in it modernized.

With no roof above him, Ky soared into the sky. Dashing around like a kid with a new toy, he was having a wonderful time. When he finally decided to look down, he could barely see the castle. Off to his left, he felt a presence that he recognized. He recognized it as his own, and he was getting closer with every passing second. He figured that in only a matter of hours, they would be coming ashore near the castle that he had just visited. After playing around in the sky, in his dream, Ky found himself drifting off to sleep once more. He couldn't figure out whether he was sleeping in his dream or in real life, but either way, he was asleep.

Chapter 4

A few hours later, Ky was awakened by Ice. To Ky's surprise the sun had risen. As foreseen in his dream, the ship was on the shore.

"Didn't sleep well, did you, Ky?" inquired Ice. "You seem startled. Everything alright?" Ky nodded. "Get sleep, when you can. You'll learn that soon enough, and you'll need some more sleep for tonight, just to warn you. And, it's easier to sleep in a bed."

"What's tonight?" asked Ky, ignoring the bed comment.

"Tonight, we are going to rescue the current leader of the empire," responded Ice.

"But aren't we anti-empire?" pondered Ky aloud.

"Well, sort of," stated Ice, "we are more along the lines of peace keepers. Just trust in my decisions. That is all I ask of you right now. It will make sense eventually. I will explain it to you, when we have more time. Right now we need to scout out the area, before we carry out this mission. And, to alleviate your concern, this Guardian is a whole lot better than the guy who wants to replace him."

Ice's voice trailed off in Ky's head because something else attracted his attention. As Ice talked with Ky, the other warriors were hauling pieces of equipment into the rafts. Ky watched the various pieces of equipment go by, wondering what each one did. After a short while, Ice gave up trying to talk to him and walked off. Ky remained, imagining how each device could be used.

Ice, Aqua, Inferno, and Hydra finished filling the raft with equipment and set the raft in the water. Hydra got in the water ahead of the raft, to make sure the path to shore was safe. After about a half an hour Hydra returned with news the path was clear. With that, Aqua set off from the ship towards shore while the rest of the warriors remained on the ship. Too curious to remain on the ship, Ky decided to take a swim and find out what the devices did.

Aqua arrived on shore only a couple minutes before Ky, but that was all the time it took him to set up. When Ky arrived, all the boxes and wires were connected. To him, it just looked like an incredible mess. Aqua saw Ky approaching and waved a warning wave to him due to the defenses Aqua had just set, but Ky didn't notice and continued towards Aqua.

"Watch out!" shouted Aqua.

The warning came just in time. Ky stopped immediately, and a small robot pulled up in front of him. It was about a foot and a half tall with two arms each equipped with two guns on them. It pointed several guns at him but didn't shoot.

"You aren't recognized in its system yet. If you take one more step, it will shoot you," informed Aqua. "It has AI like a wild animal. You have to be nice to it, in order for it to be nice to you."

"Really? Can't you just press one of those buttons on that huge piece of machinery there?" pleaded Ky.

"No, that's one of the security measures Ice took. He doesn't trust people. They make mistakes when threatened. This guy will not make a mistake. Even right now, he is updating his AI with information about you. It trusts me, and since I'm talking to you, it seems to trust you. It'll tell you when you can move," reassured Aqua.

As if on cue, the robot moved aside and said, "You may pass."

Ky cautiously walked past the robot to where Aqua was standing. All the while the robot watched him. It still didn't entirely trust him.

"What does all this stuff do?" asked Ky.

Aqua pressed a couple of buttons and responded, "watch."

A few lights flashed, four box-like containers opened and eight probes flew out of the containers. Each flew with an equal degree between them. They drifted away into the sky silently.

After asking about them, Ky learned that they were called EDs, or Extraordinary Droids. Still confused, Ky strained his eyes to see if he could spot one again, but he didn't see any.

"So," Ky started again, trying this time to get a better description, "what do they do?"

"They use micro scanners of all varieties ranging from the thermal to the..."

"In a language I speak" Ky blurted, cutting off Aqua.

"They scan the area for us," stated Aqua, "and they relay a three-dimensional image of the area that we set for them to patrol. This is very important because we can spot enemy units, traps or hazards before we operate. These droids can scan for heat, radiation, motion, energy, electricity, and many other things that we might ever need them for."

After that thorough description, Ky decided it was best if he just walked away. He walked over towards where Ice was now standing to see if he wanted to start a new conversation.

"So, what happened to Dariah and Beronith?" queried Ky.

"They were kidnapped by one of the most feared people in the world, SilverX. You're lucky you got out of that fight alive. You're also lucky that SilverX didn't bring his warriors with," scolded Ice. "Why did you try to take him on all by yourself anyway?"

"I thought the other guys were with me, I guess," mumbled Ky as he realized this wasn't quite the conversation he wanted to be in.

"Anyway, you're still alive, and you've given him something to fear," chuckled Ice, "SilverX had never before run from a battle, but next time he probably won't be alone so don't get cocky and think that you can take him on all by yourself. Keep in mind, you still lost."

"Okay"

Inferno came to the shore where Ice and Ky were standing and said, "systems up sir!"

"Thank you Inferno, suit up. You too Ky. We're going to get him."

"Who?" asked Ky.

"Ritwo."

Before Ice even said this, Ky knew whom, and he was afraid. He felt an incredible wave of fear rush throughout his body. It was the same fear he felt in his dream. He saw him and now his fears were verified. He was about to rescue someone who surely was going to try to kill Ky again, just like he had been striving to do for many years.

"What's the matter, Ky?" asked Inferno, sensing the fear in him.

"He knows me, but not in a good sense."

"Huh?" was the best description of the sound that came out of all the warriors simultaneously.

"I just realized," started Inferno, "you're that kid. You're the one that Ritwo has been hunting."

"Inferno!" barked Ice.

"I can't believe we've been traveling around with the world's most wanted person."

"Stop!" ordered Ice. "There is no proof that this is him."

"It has to be, he's the right age, his story matches up, and how else would he know and fear Ritwo. This is him," continued Inferno.

"We're doing this mission. Afterwards, we will figure all of this out. You guys are a team. We will not have, have 'this' going on," commanded Ice, "and Ky, he shouldn't recognize you through your armor. There will be no more discussion of this until I say so. Do I make myself clear, Inferno?"

"Yes, sir," he responded.

"No," Ky responded. "What do you mean he's hunting me?" So many questions just flew into his head. "How is <u>he</u> the leader of Earth? Last I saw him he was fighting the Empire in India. What did I miss? Why would I want to save someone who is hunting me? Did India win?"

Now everyone was just as confused as Ky. They all glanced around for answers. "India?" Inferno asked breaking the silence.

"Ritwo fought in India?" Ice asked. This was the most confused Ice had ever been. He was now more curious to get answers out of Ritwo than he was determined to restore order to the Earth.

Through a half hour of questions, Ky had told the warriors the entire story about how he met Ritwo in the laboratory. The warriors realized why Ritwo wanted him dead, as he was the only one who knew that Ritwo opposed the Empire in India.

Realizing they were well behind schedule after Ky's story, the warriors quickly got dressed. While Aqua, Hydra, Inferno, and Ky took off towards the base where Ritwo was being held, Ice stayed behind, at the ship, to command from a distance. Their mode of transportation for this trip began in an armored van. As soon as each warrior was in the van, Inferno started it. He pressed a button and the van started moving. Ky looked around. Something confusing for him was that he couldn't find any sort of steering mechanism.

"How does this van work?" inquired Ky.

"The EDs control it," explained Aqua, too focused on the mission to go into the subject further.

"Alright guys, you are fifty miles from the base and closing. When you are five miles away, the van will shut down and you will continue on foot. Sensors are located all over this terrain so keep moving and stay alert. No talking. Got it?" said the voice through the speakers.

"Yes," was the unanimous response from inside the van.

"One more thing, do you guys have real names?" pestered Ky.

"We do, but we can't release them for our family's security," stated Aqua.

"Oh, okay, I understand. My family's dead, so I've never thought of anything like that."

"Ky," snapped Inferno, breaking the quietness that he had maintained for most of this trip. "This is a very important mission, so how about you try to focus. If we screw this up, we will all be dead and the world will be in the hands of a crazy terrorist leader, and if somehow we don't die, I will kill you myself and collect that bounty on your head."

"*No pressure*," thought Ky. Then he thought "*bounty?*" but before he could inquire about the bounty, Ice began to talk again.

"Listen up," started the voice, "we have an ally in this fight today. They are in position with a thousand men waiting for my command. You guys need to get in and out as fast as you possibly can or you will go down with the fort."

"Okay, we're almost to the drop point; the plan is we will go in from the south. Our friend, Ya, will be taking the north. His attack should distract all the attention away from us. We will break in and search for Ritwo. Faster is better. Ky, no shit this time," explained Aqua, and after a short pause said, "Alright, everyone goes in on foot from here, pile out."

The four warriors all exited the van and headed towards the fortress in a steady jog.

"Now, listen up," said Ice over the intercom in the warrior's helmets. "You can hear me, but I don't want to hear you, so don't talk, just listen. Our ally has engaged the fort from the North, so you need to sneak in from the South and find Ritwo, the faster, the better. Ky, don't do anything stupid this time. Play it straight, don't be a hero."

At the same time that Ice stopped talking, the warriors arrived a quarter mile away from the fort at a tree line that looked as though it was created on paper with a straightedge and pencil. The line of trees was parallel to the forty-foot high wall of the fortress. The warriors could see the entire southern expanse of the fortress wall from where they stood. A door made of pure metal stood out as the only blemish on this stone wall. It was the same grayish color of the wall, but indented slightly.

With a point from Aqua, they took off towards the door. All the guards were engaged on the Northern expanse of the fort, fighting Ya. The warriors knew that the door could probably not be opened from the outside, but it would be easier to open than the wall. When they arrived at the door, they found that it could only be opened from the inside as they had originally suspected. Hydra and Inferno tried to pry the door down with no success, while Ky drifted off into a daydream, fueled by lack of sleep. In his daydream, he was brought back to the dream he had while sleeping.

Ky was startled back awake by Aqua shaking him. "Any idea?" he asked pointing to the door. Ky shook his head no without even thinking about it. He was focused on the wall, sizing it up. Completely unsure if he could make it, Ky ran at the wall, and then continued several bounds up the wall making it nearly halfway up. It was a painful landing, but Ky wasn't discouraged. He backed up to the tree line. He stood there for a couple seconds as he focused on his hands and feet. By this point, the other warriors were no longer trying to pry the door open. They were watching Ky. Once his hands and feet were as hot as he could get them, he sprinted as fast as he could at the wall. As he hoped, each step and hand placement left an imprint. He was able to scale the entire wall, with more than enough momentum.

"Climb up," he excitedly shouted once he got to the top.

From the wall, Ky could see that hundreds of soldiers were aware of his presence on top of the wall. "Never mind," he shouted, "run!"

"I'm scanning for other possible entrances," informed Ice as the warriors darted back into the woods.

Ky scaled down the wall, and chased after the warriors.

"I know another way in," announced Ky once he caught up with them.

"Really?" inquired Inferno with heavy sarcasm. "What else do you have up your sleeve?"

"I do," confirmed Ky.

"Tell us. How do you do all these things, and why do you wait until the last moment to do them? What are you hiding?"

"Stop Inferno," commanded Aqua. "We are a team. We have to trust each other. You and Ky can continue this argument after we rescue Ritwo. Right now we need a way in. Ky, you said you knew of one, where?"

"There is sewage that runs from the fort in an underground pipe. The pipe empties within a mile of here," explained Ky.

"Lead the way," said Aqua.

"Yeah do that," said Inferno skeptically. "There's always a pipe," he added sarcastically.

Ky started off in a westward direction. Hydra followed right behind him. Aqua and Inferno trailed in the back to have a conversation.

"We don't know him too well. What if he works for SilverX or Extonic? What if this is a setup?" whispered Inferno to Aqua.

"We don't know anything about him, except that he seems to be as anti-empire as they come. You saw the way he fought SilverX. He almost died fighting him. He doesn't work for either of them. But you're right, we know nothing about him, and apparently he doesn't know much about himself either," explained Aqua. "Right now, though, we need him to be right, so leave him be. After this, we'll find out who he is and everything else. You heard Ice, drop the subject."

Aqua and Inferno emerged into a marsh-like clearing with a very large pipe on one end. There was an explosion inside the pipe, and Ky emerged carrying a large metal grate.

"Here," said Ky, and he went back in.

"Alright, let's go," cheered Aqua.

All four of the warriors climbed into the pipe. It was large enough for them to stand up in, so they took off jogging down the pipe towards the fortress.

Chapter 5

Meanwhile, inside the fort, the interrogation of Ritwo and Jev has temporarily been put aside.

"Jev, Jev!" cried Ritwo. After hearing what sounded like acknowledgment, he continued, "someone's trying to rescue us. Are you able to fight?"

"Yes, master. I will always be ready to fight for you. I am willing to die for you, Ritwo"

"Good," Ritwo said reassuring himself. "If power goes down, can you take out these bars?"

"Yes, sir."

"Then we have to get out of here as fast as possible," added Ritwo.

"Right," assured Jev.

"Jev, you might be the only friend I have," whispered Ritwo.

A few seconds later, the doctor entered looking as frantic as a cat after just falling in a pool. He approached Jev and Ritwo's holding cells.

"As you both probably figured out, we are under attack by a force that appears to be trying to rescue you two. Trust me, they will fail. Right now, all I need to know is who they are. Tell me, who is trying to save you?" asked the doctor as he held out a series of pictures. "Identify them, and I will give you three hours break from the interrogation."

Ritwo saw one of the pictures and chuckled.

"What's funny?" demanded the doctor.

"The top picture. The person who is attacking you is, in fact, not a person at all," responded Ritwo.

"What do you mean?"

"He is a god."

"What..." stammered the doctor.

"It would seem that the enemy is not an ordinary army. It is Ya's holy army. You're screwed." That seemed to be all that the scientist wanted to know because he stormed out of the room.

Inside the sewage tunnel, the warriors could hear the action from above; a deafening noise echoed throughout the tunnel. One explosion, however, was much louder than the rest. The warriors looked at each other.

Aqua shouted over the noise, "the generator is down! We need to move in now!"

The power generator is the crucial part of any defense. It keeps projectiles and explosions outside of the area by means of a force field like system. Billions of nano-bots fly around at rapid speeds so they aren't visible. The generator powers them. Each one carries a charge so they can reflect anything hitting them. The generator only can be destroyed if it is overloaded by consuming too much energy or if too many nano-bots, get destroyed. When a power generator goes down, a site is basically defenseless. An exploding generator, however, is not a result of either of these.

A man by the alias of Shocon brought down this generator. He went on a mission to get inside the fort and plant explosives around the generator. Generally, everyone tries to avoid Shocon due to his lack of social etiquette, and his overall secretive nature. He spent ten years in the empire's army, receiving every possible award or medal. After he retired from the empire's army, Ya personally requested he join his holy army. To any experienced warrior, it is considered an honor to be part of Ya's army, so Shocon accepted the invitation, and he has been in Ya's army ever since. He ranks as one of Ya's private guards and is considered to be one of the most dangerous men on the planet by a large portion of the world.

About thirty seconds after the generator blew up, the four warriors arrived at another grate. This one led straight into the under works of the complex and was no longer held in place by the electronic field, so it was easily broken.

"Go!" shouted Ritwo as Jev ripped through the no longer electrified bars. It took him less than a second to get through the bars and knock out the scientist. He then proceeded to free the weakened Ritwo. As they were exiting the room, the now conscious scientist pulled out a handgun and shot Ritwo in the back of his shoulder.

"Next shot, I will kill you Ritwo," said the doctor and with a motion of the gun, Ritwo and Jev both entered back into the room. Not protected by their personal shields anymore, they proceeded to sit down in the furthest cell.

As soon as Ritwo had sat down, a knife flew through the doctor's wrist causing the gun to fall from his severed hand as they both fell to the ground. The doctor reached for the gun with his other hand, but Hydra kicked it out of his reach. The doctored gazed upward as Hydra used his fist to render him unconscious once more.

"Out!" shouted Aqua. "Let's move, Inferno and Hydra in front, Ritwo and Jev in middle and we'll take the rear. Make this fast."

They left the compound the way they had come in. They met no resistance along the way since all soldiers were needed outside. Before entering the tunnel, Aqua got on his radio and said, "Waste them, but mind our position." Then he said to the warriors, "three minutes to clear this place. They're sending in a terrestrial strike."

Ice had navigated a hovercraft into the tunnel to wait for them, so they were able to clear the area by a large distance. Three minutes later, all of them were on a boat moving rapidly away from the fort, while they watched missiles rain down on it from a satellite Ya commanded.

Until they fell asleep, Ky kept glancing over at Ritwo trying to figure out for sure if he was the scientist five years ago. Ritwo noticed him glancing over repeatedly, and put together with a dream he had while being tortured of Ky taking his place on the torture table, Ritwo was sure that this warrior was Ky.

By the time they had arrived at Ice's encampment, Ky and Ritwo were reassured who the other was, and a grudge set in. Ritwo decided he wouldn't kill Ky only because he rescued him, but he wanted to find out why Ky took part in the rescue. Still, he didn't like him. He didn't understand his hatred since, in actuality, Ky did not do much harm to his operation, and in five years, Ky had not revealed Ritwo's secret. Deep inside, Ritwo had mixed feelings towards Ky. Either he was a friend for rescuing him, or he was an enemy because he knew too much. Ky, seeing that Ritwo had not made any attempts to harm him, decided that he wasn't going to and put it out of his mind. It was still on Ritwo's mind, but for the time being, the matter was put aside.

"Alright, we sleep tonight, but tomorrow morning we start training," informed Ice. "While you train, I will get in contact with my allies to get some help with the reinstating process. It is likely that Extonic will have something prepared for when we strike. I have chosen training partners. You may not like them, but you will deal with it. Hydra and Inferno, Ritwo and Ky, and Jev and Aqua. This is the best arrangement possible. Sleep well, rise at four. Follow me to your sleeping quarters."

The six warriors followed Ice into the complex. Ritwo and Ky followed several feet behind.

"Well, I guess we're partners," said Ky nonchalantly.

"Shut up," replied Ritwo rushing ahead to talk to Ice. "He's a kid..." was all that Ky could hear of their whispers.

As Ky walked into the building, he thought back on his recent events. After many years of being stranded on an island, he was rescued, fought SilverX, and rescued Ritwo. Despite all the things on his mind, he had no troubles falling asleep, for he did not sleep well the previous night and he'd been quite active throughout the last two days creating much mental and physical fatigue. Jev, however, never slept. He sat in a chair watching over the least expected person, Ky. He was watching over Ky because he thought his master might try to do something to him in the night. Fortunately, he did not. Ritwo wasn't the murderous type despite his desire to rid himself of Ky. That night, his dreams were plagued with the remnants of the torture he'd received.

When morning arrived, nobody wanted to get up except for Jev who was already awake. For a few of the strongest, most disciplined, warriors on the earth, they were quite childish when it came to wake up call. Ky, the youngest of them all, was the hardest one to wake up. He tossed and turned for over a half an hour, but as soon as Aqua mentioned food, Ky was out of bed and to the table with miraculous speed.

Ice led the other five hungry warriors into the dining hall where Ky had already claimed half the food. The dining area itself seemed prepared for a king. There was a large buffet of food ranging from sandwiches to exotic fruits found on alien planets.

"Before you eat," started Ice as he glared at Ky, who already had a mouthful of food, "I should inform you that we will be eating four meals a day along with three snacks. There is no need to stuff yourself all at once so much that you can't move. You have a half hour for each meal and ten minutes for snack. The rest of the day is spent training."

Ky continued to eat like a pig as everyone watched. Ky realized that no one else was eating, so he looked up to see everyone watching him and said, "this is my first well prepared meal in five years. I think I've earned it."

After a half hour, Ice put his napkin down, stood up, and announced, "the meal is over. It is time to begin training."

Ky thought it was a good time for everybody to moan and did so. Everyone's attention was once again brought towards Ky. He shrugged and stuffed another forkful of eggs into his mouth.

"On that note, let's all head to the fitting room," continued Ice. He spent the next hour explaining how their workouts were going to be conducted. When he was done, the warriors were lead into their training room to being their two weeks of training.

"Ready?" Ritwo asked.

"For what?" Ky inquired.

"Fighting."

"Oh, yeah I'm ready," he said hesitantly.

Ritwo took one swing to his stomach and connected. Ky grabbed his stomach and fell over.

"No, you aren't," replied Ritwo.

Ky swung his leg at Ritwo, who was also unable to dodge or block it. Ritwo fell to the ground with pain in his shin. The two of them lay on the ground for a few minutes in pain. This is how it went for two weeks as they tried to inflict the most pain on the other in the attempt to prove a better warrior. However, since the computer that controlled the training conditions made sure each was always equal, their fights ended in a draw leading them to believe the other was always better.

Through the weeks, Ky and Ritwo developed a respect for the other because neither gave up. They would never admit it, but by the time they left, they trusted and cared for the other as a friend.

Chapter 6

Religion has always been a huge debate amongst the people of Earth; however, less than fifty years ago, what most people call the true religion revealed itself. It contained many similarities to the major religions already in existence. There was an almighty being, Marsa, but she wasn't alone in the universe. Gods were, in fact, just another species that lived in another plane of existence from humans. Demigods were able to traverse between the two planes, but could only do so on a limited basis. Gods were at war with one another. As people crave food, air and many other worldly things, gods live off of worshiping. Spiritual energy, some people call it, made gods powerful, and it hurt to lose any, yet felt good to gain. Ya was a demigod. He had only been on Earth since the time of the discovery of the religion, and as long as he was on the planet, he had no idea what was going on in his native plane.

There was one god who had grasped a larger portion of the universe than any other. His name was Darha. Some called him the devil. Darha's worshippers and demigods ravaged the universe in order to get Darha more power, but truth be told, most gods employed the same strategy. They were just worse at it.

While Ky was training at Ice's, SilverX, Dariah and Beronith came before Ya. They had requested access to the spirit plane. After explaining that Dariah and Beronith were going to slay Darha, Ya thought it was a fairly enticing deal.

"Why?" Ya couldn't help but asking. "What are you getting out of this?"

"If they slay the devil, wouldn't that absolve them of their sins?" SilverX asked. The two boys remained silent.

Still skeptical, Ya agreed to let them through specifically to Darha's world where somehow Darha managed to maintain a constant portal to the spirit world. Dariah and Beronith had killed their parents when they were seven years old. This is the sin they meant to absolve. After ensuring they knew what they were about to face, he opened a portal with a flick of his arm.

On the other side, everything seemed very blue. Crystals that appeared to be on fire on the inside shed a blue light on everything Dariah and Beronith could see. If it weren't for the eerie blue glow, the planet they were now on would have been really nice to live on. Any normal person would have already been struck with a massive headache from the light they were seeing, but because of their Archon eyes, the boys were fine.

"Welcome to Hell," mumbled Dariah as they started forward. They knew exactly where they were heading. SilverX had obtained a map of the planet at one point, and instructed Dariah and Beronith where to go.

They hadn't made it thirty feet when a figure approached them. They both drew their swords. From SilverX's instructions, they knew him as Shatnas. He was one of Darha's demigods, Guardian of Darha's temple.

Shatnas drew his own sword, a glowing blue sword that looked just like the lighted crystals that were all around. "Can I help you find your way off this world?" he asked. "The only species that can stand my light are extinct, so I presume you're looking to join your kind?" His voice was coarse and dramatic, yet his posture was unwavering. It was as though he was trying to appear more demonic than he was.

Neither boy responded to his threat. They remained still sizing him up, but they knew they had to take care of him before another demigod arrived. Dariah nodded, and Beronith took off towards Shatnas. Dariah ran faster, but in a wider arc to get behind him. Once Beronith got close enough to swing, Shatnas disappeared. He reappeared immediately in front of Dariah with one hand on Dariah's throat. With that hand, he picked up and threw Dariah at Beronith before either of them knew what had happened.

With a laugh, Shatnas explained, "you cannot kill a god. You're mortal. Whoever sent you here, sent you here to die."

"Did they?" asked Beronith challengingly as he swung his sword at one of the lighted crystals. As predicted, it exploded releasing far more light than before. Still able to see perfectly, Dariah charged and stabbed Shatnas in the stomach. In retort, Shatnas swung his sword blindly at Dariah who blocked the attack with his other sword. Still holding and twisting his sword inside Shatnas, Dariah swung down on Shatnas's sword hand removing it from his body. Quickly, he pulled a special energy gun called a sola gun from his belt, inserted it inside the hole he had created in Shatnas's stomach and fired upwards. The energy exited Shatnas's head, and Shatnas fell lifeless to the ground.

Dariah looked back with a smirk on his face, but the smile quickly left when he saw his brother lying on the ground. Beronith's arm was completely gone. The blast of the crystal had vaporized his arm. "It's fine," Beronith assured his brother in a voice that was all but assuring, but they knew they had to continue on. While they walked towards the temple, Dariah made sure there was no bleeding, but the blast had cauterized the wound as well.

Ten hours later, Dariah and Beronith returned to Earth. Beronith was nearly dead, and Dariah was in only slightly better shape. "It's done," Dariah said, as they walked onto Earth holding swords that belonged to Shatnas and Darha. Ya had no choice but to believe that what they said was true. Until he could return to the spirit world himself, he couldn't be sure.

Chapter 7

Through weeks of training, each warrior put themselves through the most physical and mental strain that they had ever felt. Every day, each one of them had wanted to quit, but they kept going because they knew that what they were about to do was that important. Some nights, they would cry, others, they would pass out without a chance to cry. Most nights, though, they would collapse before they had a chance to get to their bunks and had to be carried by the doctors that were monitoring their progress.

Constantly, the warriors' vital signs were being monitored by a team of ten highly skilled doctors, and their meals consisted of the healthiest food planned and prepared by a team of dietitians and complimented with vitamin and mineral supplements. Each day, they'd wreck their bodies only to be revived at night so they could go again the next day. Physicians constantly were working on their bones and muscles to ensure that no damage formed.

After two weeks of completely dedicated training, Ice entered for the first time. "Good job all of you. Now, you probably all feel mentally and physically, and most likely emotionally, exhausted. I have guests, leaders of specialist armies, coming over tonight. We are having a dinner with them. Before the dinner, I'll be briefing them on our plans which I will brief you on afterwards. They'd probably also like to meet who they're going to be aiding. To be honest, you all look like you desperately need a shower, so go do that and get yourselves ready for a formal dinner. I have appropriate apparel for you waiting in your rooms."

"Right away," responded Aqua and led Hydra, Inferno, Jev and Ritwo out of the training room.

"Ky?" asked Ice.

"I don't feel any stronger. I mean, I learned more ways to fight, but I thought this was supposed to make me stronger too."

"That's the point of this room," explained Ice, "as soon as you leave this room and take that suit off, you will. C'mon."

Ice led Ky out of the training room, and as promised, Ky felt immensely more powerful.

Ky enjoyed his shower far more than any of the other warriors. Aside from being sore, sweaty and surrounded by a cloud of his own body odor, Ky had not showered for five years. This was his first shower since he was twelve. He remembered the shower he took on that ordinary day. Had he known that that shower was going to be his last for five years, he would've spent much longer enjoying it, as he was now. Soaking in the warmth and the gentle feeling of the water running down his back, he ran his hands over his new body. Never had he felt this strong of muscles throughout his entire body. Everything was sore, but he enjoyed that feeling, at least this time because it was a sore that made him feel like every muscle in his body was flexed. He enjoyed his hour and a half removing layers of dirt, sweat and dead skin that had become fixed in by the sweat and dirt.

When Ky finally joined the dinner party, everyone else was seated and eating. Apart from learning martial arts and gaining strength and speed, during his two weeks in Ice's training, Ky was forced to mature several years beyond his own age. He had to hold his own against Ritwo, which meant that he couldn't be a kid anymore. He strived to be calm like Jev, strategic like Aqua and respected like Ritwo. Walking over to the table, it was obvious that he had aged as his posture and manner were strictly professional.

The dinner included the six warriors, Ice and many leaders from professional armies. Ritwo recognized Ya as one of Ice's long-time allies. More than a dozen leaders, some of which were members of the Council, sat in the dining room, all of whom were willing to pledge their armies' full support to Ice's plan to reinstate Ritwo.

No introductions were necessary at this dinner except for one person. Everyone knew of Ky, but none of these leaders had ever met him. Rumors spread throughout the world and all associated colonies about this young man. Some told of his ability to fly; others said that he was a robot bent on enslaving the world. The most common story, however, was that this young man, seventeen-years-old, was going to save the world. Almost everyone thought Ky was going to save them, and each person had a different way that he was going to do that. The rebels loved him because Ritwo wanted to capture him, and the Empire loyalists loved him now because he rescued Ritwo. He was hope. Ky, however, had no idea that anyone even knew he existed.

Ky had done nothing to gain this much attention, but people needed hope more than anything at this point. Someone with extraordinary abilities was just the person that everyone wanted to be able to save them. Ky was a superhero in the minds of billions.

"Savior," whispered one general to another as he stood in respect. Even Ice stood as all the guests stood for him. As Ky reached the table, each general extend his or her hand out to shake Ky's.

"It's good to have you on our side," Ya professed as he shook Ky's hand. It was a whole ten minutes before Ky was able to sit down after introductions. Every general there wanted Ky on their side as much as Ice wanted these generals on his.

Ice expected his guests to lose respect for Ky when they saw him eat, but he even ate with more poise. Ky had truly changed from a playful teenager, less mature than his age into a admirable warrior, deserving of respect. Ky, however, was scared, scared of the world, Ritwo, Extonic, and most of all, not living up to the high expectations that were suddenly set for him. Now that he has emerged, people demanded results.

The next morning came slowly as no one had been able to sleep. The possible outcomes of the upcoming day's events ran ferociously through everyone's heads. Even Ky, who had only recently been included in the dramatic story that is the life of the empire, understood the importance of the upcoming day.

The tension crawled beneath the sheets with him and into his veins. It made his legs restless, and his mind uneasy. It seemed like days past as he tossed and turned, even trying to sleep on the floor several times. Nothing calmed the storm inside him, nothing let him sleep.

When the warriors were brought from their rooms, Ice ran through their parts once again. After that, they loaded into flying vehicles for transportation to the Guardian Palace. Over a hundred of these crafts were loaded with twenty soldiers each. In one craft, Ky, Ritwo and Jev rode, and the others were in another.

When the warriors were almost there, they started taking fire, so they were forced to jump out of a moving vehicle. Unfortunately, troops were already closing in on their position despite the allied forces. Aqua, Inferno and Hydra stayed with the few soldiers they had with to hold their position while Ky, Jev and Ritwo headed down a secret passage.

"There's always a pipe," mocked Inferno, this time making fun of his own comment from before.

At the end of the tunnel, they emerged in Ritwo's old closet, still filled with his clothes. Exiting the closet, they were surprised to see Extonic sitting on Ritwo's desk calmly waiting for them.

"Welcome back," Extonic cheered. "I assume you're here to sign over the Empire to me, and possibly pick up your stuff."

"Never," Ritwo sternly proclaimed. The three warriors drew their weapons.

"Didn't think so," admitted Extonic. As he said this, Dariah, Beronith, SilverX and a burly looking fifth man emerged from separate hallways. "Guess my friends and I will have to do this the only slightly harder way. Tombstone, please take their weapons." The burly man started to approach them, and the three got ready to fight.

Ritwo turned to Ky. "I guess this is it. If you want to leave, I'd understand."

"If we go down," Ky started, "we go down together." The daggers Ky now held were forged from an alloy called Fuse. It was an extremely strong, yet easy to forge alloy that was used in many defensive structures. Ky focused his energy into his daggers to the point they glowed.

"My sword glows too," laughed Dariah holding the sword he took from Shatnas. Without another word, he and Beronith lunged for Ritwo. Ky tried to stop them, but was struck by Tombstone in the back. Jev turned to take on Tombstone. Ritwo watched Ky fall to the ground. Before he could help him, Beronith mercilessly thrust his sword into Ritwo's chest. SilverX, Extonic and Tombstone all took on Jev and quickly knocked him out.

Allowing Ritwo to fall to the ground, Beronith pulled his sword out and wiped it off.

"It's so hard to die," struggled Ritwo.

"No," pleaded Ky. "Don't die." Ritwo didn't respond. His eyes stared lifeless into Ky's.

Ky became irate. Flying to his feet, he forced one dagger up through Beronith's chin into his head, and his other dagger in the same way into Tombstone. Dariah finally felt fear as he stood three feet in front of Ky while Beronith and Tombstone fell to the floor.

SilverX and Extonic disappeared down the closest hallway, and Dariah readied his swords. Dariah swung at Ky, but he parried, and with both, legs kicked Dariah straight in the chest. The force was enough that Dariah flew backwards, tripping over an end table and out the fourth floor window. Seeing that there was no one else left to take care of, Ky let out his breath and relaxed. The strain he had just put his body through was too great, and when he relaxed, he collapsed completely.

Chapter 8

When Ky awoke, he was in a strange bedroom on a very large bed. The room itself was fairly large, and the furnishings looked expensive. In a corner of the room, there was a girl. "*She couldn't be over sixteen*," Ky thought.

"It's about time you awoke," said the girl. "We have to talk." Ky sensed anger in the girl's tone, so he thought it was best not to talk. "What business did you have with my father?" she demanded.

After a long, confused, pause Ky asked, "Who's your father? Wait… who are you?"

"I'm Karar. My father is Tombstone, or if you know him closer, Scott Alumin."

"Sorry, I have no idea who you are talking about," admitted Ky.

"I found you lying next to him. He was dead."

Ky's heart rate increased dramatically and his mind was filled with images of what he'd just done. He struggled to speak. "I… um… I did it," he confessed. "I killed him."

Ky expected Karar to be infuriated, but instead she stood there for a few seconds before she started laughing wildly.

"That old man got what he deserved, don't you think?" she laughed.

"What do you mean?" Ky found himself asking.

"He's a paid killer. He was paid to kill Ritwo, but I guess he ended up being killed too," Karar laughed some more. "Ironic isn't it?"

"Ironic… yeah," Ky said hesitantly.

Hungry and trying to change the uncomfortable subject, Ky asked if she had any food. She said that she did and instructed him to follow her to the dining room. It was a silent walk to the dining room. Ky spent the walk looking over her. He found her attractive. Then he realized that she was the only female he had seen in years, but continued to admire her. He also noticed that the house he was in was quite auspicious for a paid killer.

When they reached the dining area, Karar instructed a robot to provide them with food and the robot immediately left to the kitchen.

"You're the person that people have been calling 'Ky' right?" inquired Karar.

"Um… I am Ky," answered Ky. "Why? What's so special about me?"

"I've heard about you, rumors in Japan. However, you don't look exactly like the rumors say."

So many questions raced inside Ky's head that he knew he couldn't ask them all, so he started off with, "Then how did you know that I am me?"

"Just a hunch."

"I give up. What's with me? Why? How do you know me?"

"Word had spread from ranks of SilverX's army and Extonic's army that someone new works with Ice. You. You are portrayed as the answer to Japan's problems with the Empire. They saw that since you are so young, and so pure of heart, you will fight for the good of all people. Is this right?"

"Ah, I guess so," responded Ky not knowing what else to say. "But why would people think I can do that?"

Karar shrugged. "I need to go back to Japan for some things. I want you to go back with me. After all, you are practically a hero fighting with Ritwo."

Ky just remembered that he had to let Jev know that Ritwo was dead. "I have to tell Jev something," he said.

"He knows that Ritwo is dead. He's leading the empire now, so don't worry," assured Karar.

"Wait, if Japan is the rebellion, and I've been fighting with Ritwo, won't I be considered a bad guy to Japan?" asked Ky.

"No, Ritwo was never in control of the empire. The Council is in control right now, on the few things they agree on. They're practically at war with each other. Come to think of it, they are at war with each other."

"I see," said Ky even though he did, in fact, not see.

"Come with me to Japan. Many people would like to meet you," pleaded Karar.

“I’m not sure. What if I don’t live up to their expectations? What will they do to me?” asked Ky.

“When we’re there, I promise I won’t leave your side. You’ve got nothing to worry about,” assured Karar as she put her hand on Ky’s arm.

“I guess I’ll go. It’s not like I have anything else to do,” conceded Ky, now more focused on Karar’s hand than on the discussion of Japan.

Chapter 9

Later on, while on a boat, Karar and Ky continued their conversation.

"You know," started Karar, "the real reason the empire can't find Japan is it's no longer on earth."

"What?" asked Ky, startled by Karar's previous statement, "not on earth?"

"That's right!" explained Karar, "Sometime shortly after Japan's disappearance, they met an alien race that was far more advanced in space travel, but far behind in defensive weaponry. So, we traded and became good friends. Scientists from both planets started working together to create incredible inventions, including this warp to another planet, the new Japan. Its original name was FURAE, First Unified Resistance Against Earth."

Ky scratched his head in confusion and managed to blurt the words, "Wait, slow down just a bit, where are we?"

"Right now, Earth, but in a few seconds the planet, Amena," explained Karar.

"Where?" he asked again.

"Here!" exclaimed Karar as instantly the scene around the boat changed from being isolated in the ocean to a busy docking area.

Ky lost all control in his jaw as it tried its hardest to reach the floor.

"Welcome to Amena Irare, capital city of Amena, housing now over a billion Humans, Archons, and Mascien," cheered Karar.

"*Wow,*" Ky thought, "*this is incredible.*"

"With the help of the Mascien, we've built ourselves a new home," continued Karar.

"How does that portal thing work?" inquired Ky.

"Because of the conservation of Mass Energy law, we figured we could convert objects into different forms of energy with frequency to represent its atomic structure. The key to this whole teleportation mechanism is that objects accelerate slower when their mass increases, but objects with no mass, energy, accelerate at an infinite rate. Thus we can, using enough energy, send energy at a million times the speed of light. It's all physics really. The trip from earth to Amena takes only a half a second. The Masciens even have devices that don't need a receptor; they just materialize after a certain amount of time has passed. That's how they arrived on earth. I don't know how that works, but eventually I will," explained Karar

"Wait," blurted Ky, "if Japan is now this powerful, why don't they attack earth, or something."

"It isn't as simple as it seems," answered Karar, "Earth still has more people and by far more military equipment, including robots. Besides, most of the people came here to avoid conflict. They don't want to fight. They would rather run."

"Why?" inquired Ky, "if Japan is this powerful, and they have an ally that is even more powerful, why do they fear earth?"

"Who said we fear Earth?" asked a young woman who just entered the boat. "We just don't want to fight them. That's why we need you."

"What? Me? What's with me?" shouted Ky, "why has everyone been talking about me? Why does everyone want to kill me? Why me?"

"Because you have the strength to be great," replied the woman in a calm fading tone.

Ky looked over to Karar to see if she understood this new conversation and found that she wasn't even paying attention. When he looked back at this strange woman, she wasn't there, and they were suddenly docked.

"*Weird,*" thought Ky.

After exiting the boat, Ky put the previous conversation in the back of his mind as if it didn't even exist. Instead he surveyed at the dock area of this city. The first thing Ky noticed about the dock was the hundreds of people staring at him, but nobody came within three feet of him, as if an invisible bubble prevented anyone from entering Ky's comfort zone.

"They all know who you are, Ky," whispered Karar in Ky's ear.

Ky wasn't paying attention; he was too busy watching all the people as they gawked at him.

A man well-dressed in a white suit walked up to Karar, held out his arms, and said, "welcome back, Karar."

"Nice to see you again, Cycro," acknowledged Karar as she embraced him in a short hug.

Cycro then walked over closer to Ky, held out his hand, and said, "You must be Ky, then?"

"That's me," Ky replied in an I-give-up tone.

"This is Cycro," started Karar, "we work together sometimes and we are decent friends."

"Psycho Cycro," said Cycro, "that's my alias. You need any weapons, I can get them."

"No thanks," said Ky.

"Judging by the large crowd gathering here, this must be Ky, and who better to bring him to Amena than our own Karar, queen of thieves," said this new man, "I am the Guardian, or leader, of Amena. We should probably go inside somewhere before someone decides to collect the bounties on our heads. We are, after all, Earth's top four bounties if I'm not mistaken."

"Why do I have a bounty?" asked Ky after he looked at each of the people determining why they had bounties.

"You have at least a dozen, but I wouldn't worry," replied the Guardian.

"What?" demanded Ky.

"I said don't worry about it," coaxed the Guardian, "By the way my name is Damien in case you were wondering." Damien held out his hand for Ky to shake, and Ky shook it with mild hesitation.

The four of them proceeded to walk through a door that seemingly led to nowhere, but emerged in a building in the middle of the city. Ky was confused, but he assumed it was the same thing as the warp to get to the planet, only on a smaller scale.

"This is my capital building," welcomed Damien when everyone was through the portal, and he started walking down a hallway. Ky, Karar, and Cycro followed him without questioning where they were going. "Like Earth, Amena is also ruled by a council. However, this council consists of five hundred people, and each person is elected to his or her position. I am the head of the council, which means I am a figurehead for the people and I regulate the meetings. After hearing that you were coming to visit us, I scheduled a meeting, which is where we are going. The council wishes to meet with you Ky. We've heard of your accomplishments in the short time you worked for Ice, and we are impressed."

They stopped walking and gathered around a set of double doors. Karar clasped Ky's hand as if to say, "*relax*."

As Ky walked into the room, every member of the council stood just like the dinner at Ice's house only a few days before. One of the members, a middle-aged, heavyset man, walked over to greet Ky.

"I should warn you," whispered Damien, "there are those in the council, that will try to use you for their own political gain."

"Ky," addressed the council member. "Welcome to Amena. I have a favor to ask of you, but I'll wait 'til after this meeting. It's important, trust me," and the man walked back to his seat.

"His name is Alex Marxiq, and yes he is related to Sil Marxiq," said Damien while he watched Alex return to his seat without so much as glancing over at Ky.

"Can I trust him?" asked Ky.

"How do you know you can trust me?" Damien responded, and he walked to the center seat in the front of the room, leaving Ky puzzled.

Breaking the confusion in his head, Ky suddenly realized that he was still holding Karar's hand as she talked to Cycro. It felt so natural that Ky forgot about it.

"*Is this love,*" thought Ky, "*It has to be.*" Ky's palm started sweating as he held onto Karar's hand though she seemed not to notice. The thought of Karar noticing his hand sweat caused his heart rate to go up and, in turn, caused him to sweat more.

Karar noticed his heavy breathing and asked, "are you okay?"

"Huh," replied Ky, "oh, um… yeah, I guess."

"You look nervous," said Karar calmly, trying to comfort Ky. "Just relax, these politicians are nothing to fear."

"Ok," replied Ky. He should have been more nervous about the politicians at that time, but he was so nervous about Karar's hand that he forgot all about the Council.

"Ladies and gentlemen of the council," started Damien, "it is my great honor to present to you, the boy we know only as Ky." Damien pointed with his arms in Ky's direction in such a way that Ky expected a spot light to move from Damien to himself. "Come up here, Ky. The council would like to, well, bribe you, I guess, for your continued support against Earth."

Ky swallowed the nervousness in his mouth as he let Karar's hand slip from his, and journeyed towards the front podium under the two-ton weight of the gaze of five hundred councilmen and women. When he reached the front, he realized he was about to burst, for he forgot to exhale on the twenty-foot walk, and he let out the built-up supply of air from within his lungs.

Disregarding Ky's grand display of nervousness, Damien continued with the presentation. Pulling out a four-foot long sword, Damien said, "First of all, Ky, we, the council, would like the great honor of making you a knight in our society. This position is granted to soldiers who present great valor in combat in the desire to protect Amena. You have shown such quality. If you accept this position, respond saying, 'I do'."

Ky stood silently. He no longer carried the look of nervousness. It was replaced by confusion. Ky ran through the events that happened in the last few weeks trying to figure out what Damien was talking about when he said that Ky showed valor in combat.

"What say you, Ky? Do you accept?" pushed Damien. He leaned towards Ky and whispered "it's merely ceremonial, a feel-good statement for old do-nothing politicians."

"Oh, um, I do," responded Ky as confidently as one can after an awkward pause.

"Then, by the power invested in me by this council and the mighty Amena, I pronounce you Sir Kyriac, defender of Amena, knight in the first circle. Approach and receive your sword," announced Damien. Ky, still confused, did exactly as he was told and approached Damien. Damien placed the blade of the sword beneath his arm and held the handle out for Kyriac to take as he knelt down to pay respect for the newly knighted Kyriac. Ky took the sword from Damien and rested it by his side, and Damien stood up once again. "From this point forth, you shall no longer be referred to as Ky, for you shall hold with great honor the name Kyriac."

Ky had no idea what Damien was talking about, but he was impressed and slightly shocked. He still had no idea why he was important, but he liked the popularity. Then, he was brought way back to when he was twelve. Was it possible that his imaginary hero's name was Kyriac? The thought clouded his mind. When he looked at his reflection in the sword, it was clear. Ky had become Kyriac, in many ways.

"I know the council has many questions to ask of you, Kyriac, but I suppose those can wait," said Damien realizing Ky's startled appearance. Damien walked over to Kyriac, put his hand on his shoulder, and whispered in his ear, "had enough for now? Let's get out of here. I'll try to answer all of your questions, as I'm sure you have many."

As Damien, Ky, Karar, and Cycro walked out of the council room, the members shouted their questions like reporters in a press conference, though Ky heard none of it. He was still trying to figure out what was going on. Somehow, despite his awed feeling, he managed to keep his grip on his sword and, after a while, Karar's hand.

Damien quickly led the four through an array of portals until they ended up in Damien's house.

After a series of finger snaps and calling his name, Ky finally came out of his shocked state of mind. Upon doing which, he immediately dropped his sword onto the marble floor and release Karar's hand. Despite Ky's tight grip, Karar's hand had not been crushed, only hurt.

"What's going on?" asked Ky as he quickly remembered what had just happened.

"Welcome back to our world," cheered Karar, "you were in quite a daze."

"Yeah, well, I guess I was a little surprised by what just happened," responded Ky.

"It's a good thing you returned; otherwise, I was going to have to explain to the council tonight that Kyriac became petrified in my lobby," joked Damien.

"What time is it?" asked Ky.

"Lunch time, are you hungry?" inquired Damien.

It was amazing how quickly the words "lunch" and "hungry" struck Ky deep in his stomach. Ky suddenly felt starving, so he replied, "oh, yes please."

"I have food prepared in my dining hall. This way," directed Damien.

Forgetting about his sword, which Cycro picked up for him, Ky followed Damien into the dining area. Trying to remember the chivalry Ritwo taught him, Ky ate the food calmly, but still at an incredible speed. After a while, Ky looked up to see a quick glimpse of Karar's disgusted look. He immediately slowed his eating down to hopefully please her. Cycro and Damien both noticed this, and they exchanged a glace, acknowledging that the other had seen what he had seen.

After everyone appeared to be done eating, Damien asked, "well, Kyriac, you are my guest. What would you like to do until the council meeting?"

Ky shrugged, "I dunno."

"If there's anything that you want to do, let me know. Otherwise, you can stay here. Make yourself at home. I'll be here, taking care of some business. My entertainment room is down that hallway," informed Damien with a point.

Ky and Karar started heading towards the hallway when they realized Cycro wasn't with them. Karar turned around, "Aren't you coming?" she asked Cycro.

"Nope, I, too, have business," replied Cycro. "By the way, you dropped this." Cycro held out Ky's new sword.

"Oh yeah," whispered Ky as he took it from Cycro.

"It was nice seeing you again Karar, and it was nice meeting you Kyriac. I hope we meet again. If you need anything, Kyriac, let me know. I'd love to help you out," and with a wave, Cycro left.

As Ky and Karar started down the hallway, Ky pointed out, "for being a thief and smuggler, he's awfully nice."

"He isn't normally," warned Karar, "he's as ruthless and dangerous as they come. For all I know, he may be trying to get close to you so that he can get the bounty on your head. He isn't safe. He also isn't from Amena or Earth. Ever hear of the Guild?"

"Oh," responded Ky with slight disappointment in his voice. "No," he answered.

"He's a prominent member of the Guild. It's a set of colonies originally made up mostly of thieves, though it is probably now a lot safer than Earth."

As soon as Ky and Karar walked into the entertainment room, Ky noticed a large T.V. along a wall, and he rushed over to turn it on.

The first thing that appeared on the screen was an Earth broadcast. "Dr. Phillip Land of the newly founded Land Technologies announced today that he will be the first to create organic robots. Also, as the head news story the council has just announced the recreation of an Earth-wide manhunt. The person they are searching for is known only as Ky. This is what he looks like." A picture of Ky appeared on the screen. Ky felt a sudden feeling of despair setting in throughout his body. The news continued, "The body of the suspect is wanted preferably intact, but as long as it is identifiable, the person who kills or captures him will receive four hundred billion seed. This is the largest bounty ever..." The voice faded off as more despair and fear set into Kyriac's mind.

"It's okay Kyriac," said Damien from the hallway entrance. "The

Earthen bounty hunters are horrible. They still haven't caught me, and until now, I was the highest bounty out there. Trust me, you'll be fine."

"Really?" asked Ky with no other words coming to mind.

"Yeah, besides they can't get you with your new armor. There isn't an Earth weapon that can penetrate that," comforted Damien. "Come on, I've decided you probably need a shower and a nap before you meet the council again. That way you'll look more composed and intimidating. Maybe they'll be gentle if they're scared."

"Alright," agreed Ky, and Damien led him to the shower and showed him where the guest room was along the way.

"Wear your armor to the meeting, too," suggested Damien. "Intimidation can only help."

Ky enjoyed his third shower since he left his island, and after his shower, Ky fell asleep so quickly, he didn't have time to let the covers find his torso.

Chapter 10

"Wake Up Kyriac!" shouted Damien on his sixth attempt to wake Kyriac up.

Since yelling had proved useless, Karar walked over, threw the sheets off and shook Kyriac's foot violently. Seeing that Kyriac didn't even change his breathing or move slightly, she picked him up and threw him on the ground. This abruptly woke him.

"Hi?" Kyriac said hesitantly wondering why he was on the ground and why Karar and Damien were standing over him.

"Get up and dressed," commanded Damien. "We've been trying to wake you for quite some time, but you wouldn't wake up."

Kyriac shrugged, and stood up. He scratched his head and while doing so, saw his armor laid out neatly on a dresser, causing him to remember the meeting he was going to. Damien and Karar left to allow Kyriac to get dressed. When Kyriac emerged, he was wearing a full set of white armor, including a cloak and helmet.

"You don't need to wear the helmet, but bring it with," informed Damien. When Kyriac removed the helmet, he now had white hair instead of his normal brown. It was the same medium length, but seemed crisper compared to its previous oily look. Kyriac looked respectable and well kept. In his white armor and new white hair, Kyriac's green eyes stood out drawing attention to them, giving a mystical feeling about him. Up until now, Karar hadn't noticed how attractive he was; now, she couldn't look away.

Kyriac glanced at Karar to find her staring at him, so Kyriac half-smiled. Karar realized she was staring at him, and quickly turned away blushing a bright shade of red. Kyriac didn't notice her blushing because he was busy noticing the dress she was now in. With her looking away, he took the opportunity to completely look over her. Her hair was much longer than he had thought, extending halfway down her back. It was a shiny shade of brown, straight hair that looked soft if only Kyriac had the opportunity to feel it. Her skin wasn't pale, but it wasn't tan either; rather, it had a rosy tint and fair complexion. Her eyes were the most drawing feature. They were brown, but entrancing to Kyriac. She had a couple freckles just beneath her eyes that were hardly noticeable if the person looking wasn't looking as closely as Kyriac was now.

"Right," was the first thing Damien could say after looking at Kyriac's hair, "Kyriac, perhaps you should look in a mirror."

"Why?" asked Kyriac as he darted back into his room to examine himself in a mirror. It took less than a second for Kyriac to answer his own question. He touched his hair to see if it was an illusion.

"The armor is supposed to bind with whoever uses it," stated Damien. "I just didn't expect anything like that to happen."

Damien thought that Kyriac was displeased by the way his hair now looked, but Kyriac liked it. He ran his hand though his hair once more to see the way it moved. It returned to its original place as if something held it there. His hair waved slightly from Kyriac's own sway, but only the sort of waving that skyscrapers do; never too much, just enough to be noticed.

"Sweet," reacted Kyriac.

With a shrug, Damien said, "Let's go, we don't want to keep the elderly waiting." Kyriac chuckled at Damien's remark, relieving a small fraction of the stress that was built up within him.

"Why did I look away?" Karar asked herself. "What is it about him? He's just a boy. Get a grip, Karar; don't screw this up."

Kyriac followed Damien back to the portal in Damien's lobby as Karar followed just far enough behind that Kyriac wouldn't notice she was there.

When they reached the portal, instead of going through, Damien stopped and remained silent for ten seconds, and Kyriac looked back to see Karar staring at him again. Again, she turned away quickly.

"Change of plans," announced Damien.

"Huh?" Kyriac sounded.

"Ice's base was attacked. Kyriac you need to get back to Earth, and see Jev, as fast as possible."

"What about the council?" asked Kyriac.

"That'll wait. Right now we need to figure out what's going on back on Earth, and you're the person to do it," responded Damien.

"Um..." started Kyriac.

"Let's go," commanded Damien before Kyriac could continue. Damien walked through the portal, and Kyriac followed.

"Get a grip, Karar," thought Karar, as she let out the air she held since Kyriac looked at her again and followed through the portal.

They emerged in the port that Kyriac and Karar arrived at earlier that day.

"Sorry it couldn't last longer. It was a pleasure to meet you, Kyriac," said Damien. "You two hurry to Jev. He'll tell you what to do next."

Kyriac shook Damien's outstretched hand, and Karar and Kyriac got onto Karar's boat. Karar fired up the engines, plotted the course into the computer, and settled in next to Kyriac for their fifteen-minute ride back to Earth.

Chapter 11

As the shore approached, Kyriac said the first thing since the boat ride began. "I think someone is waiting for us on shore," he said.

"What?" panicked Karar as she looked to see for herself.

Sure enough, the shapes of two men were visible standing on the shore just beyond where the waves reached. Karar grabbed a circular device, about two inches in diameter, and she pulled a strap out from the bottom side and slide in onto her right arm. Kyriac recognized the piece of equipment Karar was using as one of the personal shields that the council had given him. Following suit, Kyriac grabbed the other one and found that it attached right to the arm of his armor.

When they were within one hundred yards, Karar recognized the two people standing there. They were both bounty hunters: Jake Arab and Rocco Smith, hired for large amounts of money to kill away Earth's problems. They were chosen by Earth because they were robots, ruthless and error free.

Sensing tension in Karar, Kyriac asked, "Who are they?"

"Bounty hunters," she replied, "and good ones."

"How good?" inquired Kyriac with the tone in his voice such that Karar knew he planned on fighting them.

She knew she couldn't stop him, so she said, "they're robots. Don't wait for them to make a mistake, 'cause they won't. They are flawless with their many guns and solas, so fight them short-ranged; it's your best chance. You can outrun them, but not their guns."

"I'll stay and fight," informed Kyriac. "You run."

"I'm not leaving you to fight them alone," responded Karar. "I can fight, too."

Kyriac would've continued trying to convince Karar not to fight, but Karar saw that one of the robots pulled out his sola and lined up with the boat. She grabbed Kyriac and pulled him over the edge. Within a second, the boat was engulfed in a wave of energy.

When Kyriac and Karar returned to the surface, there was only steam, no boat. The other robot pulled out his sola. Kyriac grabbed Karar and threw her into the air away from him. Simultaneously, he pushed off in the water swimming in the other direction. The sola shot flew between them while Karar was still in the air. Completely unprepared for what just happened, Karar swallowed a large amount of salt water in her attempt to breathe.

When Kyriac reached the surface of the water, he took off in an attempt to run in a half-run, half-swim fashion. Jake Arab saw Kyriac coming, pulled out a handgun, and fired one shot, which hit Kyriac's chest, slightly to the left where his heart was. The bullet didn't penetrate Kyriac's new armor, but it did cause Kyriac's torso to lose momentum. His legs kept going just as fast as they had, so his legs flew out into the air until Kyriac was parallel to the water. To correct, he arched his back and flipped into the water perpendicular to the surface as if he was diving. He then proceeded to kick his legs like a dolphin powering through the water. When the water became too shallow, he soared out and swung his fist at Rocco Smith. The robot gracefully slid out of the way and hit Kyriac with his elbow on the middle of Kyriac's spinal cord. Kyriac belly-flopped to the ground and lost all breathing ability for an instant. Then the other robot pulled out a knife, tilted Kyriac's head upward, and slid the knife in front of his throat.

Coming to grips with what just happened, Kyriac started coughing and gasping for air.

"You are under arrest," stated the perfectly human voice of Jake Arab, "for treason and murder in the highest degree."

"We have every authority to execute you, so please come peacefully," informed Rocco Smith, the robot not holding the knife to Kyriac's throat.

Suddenly, a sword protruded from the chest region of Jake Arab and was pulled out just as fast as it had entered. Jake quickly stood up, despite the wound, and slashed his knife. Kyriac recognized the sword as his own, so he looked behind him expecting to see Karar. Karar, however, was not there. It looked like Jake was slashing at nothing, but when he completed the slice, Kyriac heard Karar groan in pain, and there was blood on Jake's knife.

Kyriac wasted no time, and swung his legs around into Rocco's legs. Rocco lost his balance and fell over. While falling, he tried to punch Kyriac, but Kyriac grabbed Rocco's hand and sat up. With incredible speed, he put his other hand through Rocco's head.

Meanwhile, Jake threw his knife into Kyriac's elbow with enough force that it pierced the armor. With the knife still protruding from Kyriac's elbow, his hand continued on its path into and through Rocco's mechanical skull.

Jake jumped forwards to finish Kyriac off, but instead, he dove into the invisible sword that the invisible Karar held. Karar turned off her cloak field to show Jake she held a sola. With a click, whatever emotions this robot could feel were removed and Jake was no more.

Kyriac rolled over onto his back, in extreme pain, to see Karar standing over him protecting him. Karar turned around to see if Kyriac was all right. They made eye contact again, but this time Karar didn't look away. Even though he was in pain, Kyriac managed to smile at Karar as if to say, "thank you, I'm alright," even though he was not.

"I'll call someone to get a ride," informed Karar after pulling her gaze away from Kyriac's eyes. She walked over to a nearby tree, and stood on the other side of it.

Kyriac quickly and painfully took off his upper armor and undershirt. Before he put back on his armor, he used his undershirt as a sling to prevent his arm from moving. After he was done, Karar came back over.

"Someone's coming," she informed. She had been watching, without Kyriac knowing. She asked, "are you hurt?"

"Not bad," he lied, "you?" Karar felt where she had been slashed. Kyriac could see the blood still coming out of the wound on her side. "You need to fix that up," warned Kyriac disregarding his own problems.

"It'll be fine," assured Karar.

Being stubborn, Kyriac continued, "I can close it."

"It's fine," pushed Karar.

"Trust me, please," pleaded Kyriac.

Karar gave in. "Alright," she said, and she walked closer to Kyriac. She didn't like the idea of more pain, but she liked the fact that Kyriac was caring for her. Kyriac pulled out his dagger and started running energy through it. It heated up quickly.

"This will hurt," he warned, and he pressed the flat side of the dagger against the wound, cauterizing it. Karar clenched her fists and squeezed her eyes closed. When she opened her eyes again, she realized she had clenched her fists around Kyriac's good arm, and she immediately let go, not because she was afraid of hurting him, rather she felt awkward touching him. She looked at her wound. It had stopped bleeding, but it hurt worse than it did before.

"So," started Kyriac, trying to break the tension, "how'd you go invisible like that?"

"Oh, I stole that when we were in Amena," responded Karar, "I thought it could be useful."

"You were right," laughed Kyriac.

"It's hard to use, though. I couldn't see what I was doing," she explained. "I had to do it all by feel. That's why I had to leave the cloak to shoot. Otherwise, I had no way of aiming."

"I think I'm going to listen to you from now on," stated Kyriac, "those guys were tough. If it weren't for you, I'd probably be dead or something."

"No you wouldn't," predicted Karar. Shortly after saying it, Karar regretted doing so. "*Stupid,*" she thought to herself.

Kyriac, unsure how to respond to Karar's comment, remained silent until their ride arrived. Karar realized that she killed the conversation, so she started salvaging through what Rocco Smith had. She took what she could carry and left the rest for whoever might pass by.

Shortly after Karar finished sorting through Rocco Smith's weapons, a kid arrived in a helicopter that was slightly smaller than the ones that Ice used.

"Come on," Karar said, and they got in the helicopter. "Thanks for picking us up, Fly."

"Anything for you, Raider," replied Fly, as he lifted the helicopter off the ground and headed toward Jev's palace.

Chapter 12

Jev greeted Kyriac as he arrived. "Welcome Kyriac, won't you come inside. We have matters to discuss," gestured Jev.

"Right to business," Kyriac mumbled as he followed Jev inside. Karar, too, followed after she waved for Fly to leave.

Before they entered, Jev stopped and said, "please don't steal anything, Raider," while looking straight at Karar, and, with that said, he opened the door and led them in. The three of them proceeded through the house until they reached Jev's office.

"That arm looks really bad," Jev pointed out.

"It's not bad," Kyriac lied, again.

"You can't lie to me," stated Jev. "However, it's not so bad that the microbes in your blood can't fix it. You did the right thing by putting your arm in that sling, otherwise..."

"Wait," blurted Kyriac, "what microbes?"

"Surely Ice," started Jev, but he paused for a second to think. Then he started again. "Warriors in armies are injected with microbes, so that they heal at a rapid pace. I guess I just assumed because of your nature you already had them." Jev pressed a button on his desk and spoke louder, "Bring Kyriac a microbe needle." Then he addressed Kyriac again, "You need this, or that bone will take months to heal. And we don't have months."

"Does it have to be a needle?" Kyriac asked.

"Huh, why not?" responded Jev.

"I don't like needles," admitted Kyriac.

"But you will fight with swords and knives?" Jev pointed out. "You got stabbed with a knife. This'll be quick, and you need this."

As if on cue, a man carrying a needle walked through the door. Kyriac stepped back bumping into a chair. Following the man with the needle, Karar walked back into the room, though neither Jev nor Kyriac noticed that she had left. She walked directly to Kyriac, grabbed his hand with one hand, and put her other hand on his shoulder. Kyriac glanced at Karar, but his attention was quickly brought back to the needle. He clenched his still working fist, squeezing Karar's hand until it broke. Kyriac heard the crack from Karar's hand, and he realized what he had done. Karar cried out in pain.

"I'm… I'm sorry," Kyriac pleaded for Karar's forgiveness.

The doctor found this an opportune moment and stuck the needle into Kyriac's broken arm. Kyriac swung his fist around to punch the doctor, but Jev instinctively grabbed Kyriac's arm, spun it around behind Kyriac's back, and kicked the back of both of his knees. Kyriac landed on his knees before he realized what had just happened. He let his thoughts gather.

"That could've gone better," mumbled Jev.

The doctor didn't wait until he was dismissed; he wanted to get away from Kyriac as quickly as possible. Sensing that Kyriac regained control of himself, Jev let him stand up.

"Your arm will heal in two days max now that you have those microbes," informed Jev, "How 'bout you, Raider, how are you?"

"I'll live," groaned Karar. When Kyriac was caring for her, she formed grand thoughts that he would never let her come to harm. Now that he hurt her like this, she felt betrayed. She didn't understand how she could have these mixed emotions in such a short period of time.

"The reason you are probably here is because Ice's encampment was attacked," started Jev back to the order of business. "The council ordered it. They're all blaming you and Ice for Ritwo's death. I know SilverX is controlling the council, but politically, I can do nothing. I need you, Kyriac…" Looking over Kyriac's armor, he continued. "So they knighted you? They're going to call upon you to fight for them now," warned Jev. "If you want to make sure Ice and the others didn't die for nothing, here's what you need to do. A fighting tournament is coming up. This is the biggest event of the year. All the big names will be there, if not to fight, to gain political power. Since you have a bounty on you, you cannot enter the tournament, but you can sneak in and hide in the crowd. SilverX must lose this tournament. I don't know how you might stop him, but you need to. Understand?"

"No," responded Kyriac as he shook his head. "What's it matter if SilverX wins?"

"This tournament is like a political rally. The better one does in the tournament, the more highly respected and famous he is, thus giving political power. I believe that in conjunction with the tournament, SilverX's army will make another attempt at the guardian thrown, so Ya and I will not be at the tournament."

"I just don't understand how a fighting tournament increases political power," admitted Kyriac as he tried to process what Jev was telling him as fast as he was hearing it.

"This tournament has been around for over three hundred years. It is an independent entity from our government, and has remained neutral forever; therefore, everyone respects its purity. There are a lot of fans of the tournament, so whoever controls those fans has a massive group of people that they can use for political power. SilverX is also campaigning that only the strongest person should be Guardian. Now he's trying to prove that he is that person. If he doesn't win, he can't hold up to his own expectations of Guardian," informed Jev.

Karar was so quiet that Jev and Kyriac hadn't noticed that she slipped out of the room and came back. "I can help," she suggested.

"How do you suppose you'll help? You're a thief, not a mercenary," reminded Jev.

"No, but my father was," Karar pointed out, "and he taught me how to fight, and I have this." Karar waved her new hand device to show Jev.

"What is it?" asked Jev.

Karar activated it and turned completely invisible.

"*That's how she disappeared from the room without me noticing,*" thought Jev.

Kyriac felt Karar brush past him, and she reappeared two inches in front of Jev. "I can attack him while he's in a battle, and Kyriac... er, Kyriac, can't because SilverX will know he's there. He steps too loud."

Kyriac was puzzled at how Karar knew this about him when he, himself, did not, especially since she had known him for a very short period of time.

Still skeptical of Karar's motive, Jev asked, "What's in this for you?"

"Jev," Karar said as she moved closer to him, "I'm doing this for him," she whispered.

Jev didn't trust Karar, yet he conceded, "I'm not going to tell you that you can't attack SilverX in the ring. If she fails, though, Kyriac you must stop him, alright?"

"I think so," replied Kyriac, with no question this time, although Jev waited for one.

Hearing no question from Kyriac, Jev said, "You may stay here for a while, if you need to. I'm willing to bet you're tired." Jev led them to their rooms. "The rest will allow the microbes a chance to work."

Kyriac nodded and quickly realized he was exhausted, but from all the zone changes, he had no idea what time it was. Once his head hit the pillow Kyriac was asleep, but Karar stayed up a while to think about Kyriac and why she cared for him.

"*Why is he special?*" she pondered. "*If I turn him in, I can collect his bounty. He's just a thing, a person, a bounty to collect.*" Karar left her room to look at Kyriac, see if her answers were in there with him. "*He's so peaceful lying there. I can't do this anymore.*"

"What are you doing?" asked Jev, now beside her.

"I don't know," responded Karar, unconsciously. Frustrated with herself, she continued, "I don't know what I'm doing anymore."

"One minute you're trying to impress him, the next you're saving him. Now you're standing over watching him as he sleeps," Jev outlined. "Are you in love with him?" Karar didn't respond, so Jev continued. "It seems like everybody is. That's the magic behind who he is. I don't know why, but everyone seems to love this kid. The only difference between you and everyone else is that he seems to be attached to you too. I warn you, don't hurt him, and be careful what you ask of him. He just might do it," warned Jev.

"You don't need to worry about me. I couldn't stand to see him get hurt," assured Karar.

Chapter 13

As Kyriac and Karar slept, Jev met secretly with Dariah. Jev was surprised Dariah agreed to meet with him at all, so he was extremely precautious once he arrived.

"Dariah," Jev started. "First of all, it is a pleasure to meet you, but I wish the circumstances were better. I need to know what happened in the fight, and why you are working for SilverX."

"In the fight, that kid, Kyriac, killed my brother," replied Dariah.

Jev hoped the council was wrong that Kyriac killed Beronith, but hearing Dariah say so convinced him. "I see," he solemnly spoke.

Dariah answered his next question without being asked. "Because Beronith killed Ritwo." Dariah unsheathed his sword, and Jev stepped back to prepare for combat.

"Don't do this Dariah, we don't need to fight," Jev pleaded trying to talk his way out of fighting.

Dariah held his sword out in front of him with both arms fully extended and said, "Save your pleas, I'm not going to kill you, nor will I kill again." Jev relax slightly, but remained cautious. Dariah continued, "I have seen, first hand, the effects of fighting, and, through the cost of my brother's life, I have come to realize how painful it can be. Take my sword, Jev, and keep it safe. As long as you have my sword, I shall never fight again."

Jev was caught off-guard. He had not expected Dariah to give up fighting just like that. He assumed that Dariah and Beronith were creatures of pure evil, though at this moment, Dariah was more humane than any human. All Jev could say was, "What?"

"I'm done. I shall no longer kill. I only hope that Kyriac, SilverX, and all those other people who wage this war realize what I have," Dariah said.

"What did you realize?" inquired Jev.

"Those people you kill," said Dariah as his voice cracked, and it became harder for him to speak. "Those people that die have families and people that care about them, and as long as people keep on fighting, there will always be those who oppose them. They think they are fighting for peace, but peace can never be achieved by them, especially not by Kyriac."

"How can you think that way?" insisted Jev. "These people are fighting because they believe in something so great that they are willing to sacrifice their lives. Isn't something that great worth fighting for?"

"No," replied Dariah without the sadness in his voice. "All this fighting has accomplished is more fighting. Nothing ever ends. I too have seen Amena. There is no war there. They could wipe out Earth if they chose to, but they'd rather live hidden, if that means they live in peace. Did you know there are worlds out there where there is no murder?"

"What about this empire? Was Crotonee fighting for nothing? Did he also accomplish nothing?" pressed Jev.

"This empire only leads to a much larger war," warned Dariah. "This war is all I see in my dreams. Fighting must be stopped, and during the fighting tournament, I will stop it."

"What war? What are you planning?" Jev pleaded. "What are you talking about? None of this makes any sense."

"You will see, in time," answered Dariah. "Where is the kid right now? I need to speak with him. This is the real reason I am here."

"He is here, sleeping," responded Jev. "Why do you need to see him"?

"He must know that I am not his enemy, and that Beronith's life was not as worthless as he thinks. He is the key to stopping all fighting. I must persuade him first."

"I will let you speak with him after the tournament," conceded Jev. "He has to stop SilverX from winning the tournament. After that, he can stop fighting."

"SilverX will not win that tournament. That is already taken care of," informed Dariah. "Nor will his army attack you. You'll see."

"You aren't making any sense, Dariah," admitted Jev.

"You will see, and I can wait until after the tournament to speak with Kyriac," said Dariah. "But believe me when I tell you, SilverX will not win this tournament. Arcadius will. I will see you again soon, Jev." Dariah left the office leaving Jev in a pool of questions. He, though very intelligent, had no idea what Dariah was doing. He knew this wasn't a ploy of SilverX's because Dariah left his sword behind and could've killed Jev if he wanted to. Nothing that just happened made sense. "*What just happened*," he thought. "*What are you planning to do, Dariah?*"

As soon as Dariah was gone, Karar appeared standing in the corner of Jev's office. Jev didn't notice until she said, "So that's Dariah."

Jev was startled by her sudden presence. "Why are you here?" he exclaimed.

"I'm not sure if that was a question or just you being startled," mocked Karar.

"Why are you in here?" Jev asked stubbornly.

"Believe it or not, I was here to protect you in case Dariah tried attacking you," replied Karar. Jev had his doubt, and he showed it well. "So are you going to tell him?" she asked.

"Tell who what?" asked Jev.

"Tell Kyriac what happened and what Dariah said," responded Karar.

"Why would he need to know?" asked Jev.

"In this last day," Karar started, "I've come to realize how politics work. The goal is to have as many people eating out of your hand as possible. You do this with the guardian position, and as long as people believe in the guardian, you have power. If someone wins the fighting tournament, for example, people believe they are powerful, and thus flock to them. Now in the case of Kyriac, millions of people believe he will answer all their troubles, so whoever controls Kyriac has a lot of power. That's why you, Damien, and even Ice have been hiding any shred of truth from him. It's all politics, right?"

"What's your point?" inquired Jev.

"My point is," continued Karar, "you have to stop controlling him like a political pawn. Let him know everything, or I will, and you know that if I tell him, you will lose every chance of keeping him as an ally."

"My intent was never to use him," explained Jev. "I am trying to protect him. Can you imagine what would happen to him if he suddenly gained all that power? In time, I will let him know, trust me."

"Only if you do the same and trust me," bargained Karar as she walked out the door with her point floating in Jev's mind.

Chapter 14

"Sir, we have the list for the tournament," announced one of SilverX's advisors as he walked through the door to see Extonic and SilverX sitting at a table sipping wine. "It looks good for you. You and Extonic should meet in the final round as planned."

"What about that kid?" asked SilverX.

"He's not in here as a scheduled match. He might still walk on, but I don't think he can enter the tournament with that bounty," explained the advisor.

"Good," mumbled SilverX.

The advisor continued, "In the first round, both of you will face your walk-ons. Then SilverX will face Sinerias. He's a captain in the empire's army, but he's not strong enough for this. Extonic will face Ma. From what I've gathered, Ma is a farmer in Southern Africa, again an easy match. In the third round, SilverX, you will face Shocon, since Aqua won't be there, another military man, but this one is a little stronger. However, at his age, he should be nothing. Extonic, you will face either Dice or Bounid. Both are just kids trying to make a name for themselves, but neither of them knows what they're doing. Then, in the final round, you will face each other, and after a long and impressive battle, SilverX will win."

"Only after I win, will you get paid," added SilverX.

"Don't worry SilverX, you can count on me," assured Extonic. "I want this as bad as you. I don't even care about the money."

"I want Dariah there, in case Kyriac shows up," demanded SilverX.

"I'm sorry, sir, we don't know where Dariah is," explained the advisor with hesitation.

"What!" exclaimed SilverX.

"He never returned from his last mission," explained the advisor. "I sent out agents to find him, but they've had no success."

"Did Jev kill him?" whispered SilverX to himself.

"No sir, we checked with Jev already," continued the advisor disregarding that SilverX wasn't talking to him. "Jev had his sword, and he said that Dariah gave up fighting because of his brother's death."

"Tell your agents that when they find him, they should kill him," commanded SilverX. "He's just a pawn. We can make a new one."

"I don't understand, sir," admitted the advisor.

"You don't have to," smirked SilverX. "If he won't fight, he's no good to us. Extonic, make yourself useful and go tell those science geeks our situation. And, you go inform your agents. The quicker he's gone the better. Wait… on second thought, tell your agents to track him. I want to know where he is at all times. We'll let his cyber kill himself." Extonic and SilverX both laughed slightly as though there was some hidden joke that only they understood. The advisor laughed also, even though he had no idea why he was laughing.

"Go!" ordered SilverX suddenly to the advisor, and the advisor scampered out of the room.

"We only need one," informed Extonic.

"I know, but this one will be a quick one just for the purpose of destroying Dariah. Damage control, you see. Then he'll die in some honorable battle," explained SilverX as he laughed again. "And then we'll keep the favor of having had him on our side, and in death, he'll keep all his persuasion over people."

"After this tournament," started Extonic, changing the subject, "will we be powerful enough to overthrow the council?"

"We already control half the council," explained SilverX, "but that's not what we want. We want to dissolve the council entirely, and have one ruler that we can control."

"But who could we control like that?" laughed Extonic because he knew that answer. He was just setting SilverX up to say it.

"Why the cyber, of course," laughed SilverX.

Extonic poured two glasses of wine, and raised his up in the air. "Two weeks," he cheered.

SilverX grabbed his glass, and said, "to power." They clinked glasses together continued plotting as the night continued.

Chapter 15

For four days, Kyriac and Karar stayed at Jev's house, and for four days, that house remained silent. Jev was normally quiet, but Kyriac and Karar seemed to avoid each other. All three of them ate, slept and worked on different schedules. Only once did Kyriac and Karar eat at the same time, and during that meal, not a word was spoken. It was incredibly awkward between them. The crushes they had on each other reminded Jev of two kids in middle school approaching each other for the first time, not knowing how to break the silence.

Kyriac spent most of his time awake working out. He'd spend half the day fighting invisible opponents in Jev's courtyard. Jev was right about the nanites; they fixed his arm in only two nights. Kyriac didn't know what drove him to make him train. All he knew was that when he was fighting, he felt relaxed and unaffected by what was happening in the world, and what happened five years ago. Aside from the physical training he went through, he also taught himself how to fight with the sword he'd received, and he practiced with his daggers simultaneously until he could efficiently wield all three at the same time. Then he practiced more, just to make sure.

Karar spent her days working on the cloak field and the sola guns she had stolen from the bounty hunters. Despite her upbringing, Karar was brilliant. Most people assumed that because she was a thief, she was dumb; however, her intelligence exceeded almost all the people on Earth. A small few, including Dr. Land, Jev, and the deceased Ritwo, were more intelligent than she was. However, in her area of expertise, Mascien technology, she was, by far, the best on Earth, probably because nobody had quite the access that she had to those technologies. Sola guns had originally been an Earth technology, but Masciens studied them and created better kinds, though the main problem with them remained, the heat generated. After a sola is fired, it could take upwards of an hour to cool down before it can be fired again, thus it was pretty much a one-shot gun. Versions, called sola cannons, were created on Amena that cooled down much faster, but they were massive by comparison.

Now Karar was using the miniature cloak generator to, not only hide the gun, but also disperse the heat produced by it. The concept behind the cloak was that it removed all light waves that were affected by the area within it and dispersed them into a black hole near the Mascien solar system, which the Masciens used for energy. With a few modifications, Karar was able to disperse the large amount of heat instead of the visual waves. She figured she needed to see the gun in order to aim it anyway, so the loss of the cloak field was not disappointing. She did the same thing to her other sola and created two new cloak generators, one for herself and the other for Kyriac.

Jev spent his four days attempting to fortify his mansion. Kyriac and Karar would enter the dining room to find a new weapon stash, or walk down a hallway and get shot at by a turret. It appeared as though Jev was losing control of his mind.

"He's getting weird," Karar said as she came out of cloak in Kyriac's doorway.

"Why do you do that?" Kyriac demanded, startled.

"Do what?" she asked.

"Go invisible and spy on people," Kyriac replied.

"I didn't spy, I just came down the hall," Karar answered. "I was testing this one out. Here, it's yours." She threw the device to Kyriac. "It's easy to use. Press the button, you're invisible. Press it again, you're visible. I haven't tested the battery life yet, but I wouldn't use it excessively. It might be useful someday." Karar walked away, and as she did, she realized that had been the first conversation they'd had in four days.

In Siberia at SilverX's current base, this was one of the busiest days ever. Servants were waiting on SilverX and Extonic to be sure they were ready for the tournament, while the military prepared and tested their equipment, getting everything organized so that it may be deployed at a moment's notice once SilverX wins the tournament. SilverX, however, was still worried by the missing Dariah. He had essentially brainwashed Dariah so that he would obey everything SilverX told him to do, but he had somehow escaped SilverX's grasp. Now, SilverX had no idea what he was up to, and in his mind, Dariah was the most dangerous person on the planet, not only because he was a powerful fighter, but because he knew things about SilverX that could ruin his plans.

Dariah hid and waited, just outside, for SilverX to leave. He didn't quite know how he was going to stop SilverX's army, but he'd promised Jev that they weren't going to invade. He had nothing with him, no weapons or explosives, nor did he want any. Having a weapon would only further tempt Dariah into killing someone, which was exactly what he was trying to avoid. He knew, first hand, what it felt like to lose someone close. Beronith was so close to Dariah, and he cared so much. He died through Kyriac's anger. Somehow, he planned, he would stop this attack without taking a single person's life; he would rather lose his own.

SilverX and Extonic had to leave for the tournament to check in and watch the last few rounds of the walk-on tournament to make sure there were no surprisingly strong walk-ons. The walk-on tournament involved thousands of people each year and lasted for weeks, so, by the time the actual tournament arrived, the walk-ons were tired and generally injured. This made the first round of the tournament an almost guaranteed win for those pre-entered. The last eight walk-ons are given an hour to heal, and then each walk-on is entered in against one of the fresh pre-entered fighters. Those fighters were given plenty of rest between fights having each round start six hours after the previous round with the first at six in the morning and the final fight at midnight.

Kyriac and Karar, fully armed, snuck into the tournament, at about the same time SilverX arrived, under the protection of their cloak generators. They arrived just in time to watch Arcadius, one of the walk-ons, defeat the last of SilverX's warriors, and instead of going off and getting ready for his next match, he stood by the arena, watching the other matches, waiting for his next bout. Thirty-one matches later, he won again, then again after fifteen, putting him in the tournament against Extonic. Each match had to have taken a lot out of him, so Extonic was not afraid. SilverX, however, noticed he was calm and quiet, and though most fighters were quiet and controlled, the extent of Arcadius's control during and after a fight disturbed him.

After the walk-on rounds were finished, the announcer's disembodied voice announced, "The preliminary rounds are finished. The qualifiers are, in this order, Arcadius, Marx, Eddy Nogly, Torus, Angel, Shansui, Rathenal, and Marshall Winest. Congratulations to those who qualified and good luck. We will now take a one hour break for these fighters to recover, and we will start the tournament at six."

Kyriac and Karar met at the spot they had chosen before and uncloaked. Along the way to the meeting spot, Kyriac bumped into several people and tripped over himself twice. Like Karar had predicted, she was better with the cloak than he was.

"*Dariah might be right*," thought Karar after she heard the name 'Arcadius.' "New plan," she said to Kyriac when he finally appeared. "We wait to take out SilverX."

"What? Why?" asked Kyriac.

"I overheard something from Jev. I think we have a friend in the tournament that will stop him," explained Karar. "Watch Arcadius. If he gets out before fighting SilverX, then we have to take him out."

"Who's Arcadius?" questioned Kyriac.

"I don't know, but he's supposed to stop SilverX," answered Karar.

Since he never fully understood what was going on, Kyriac decided to drop the subject. "Let's go get a good spot to watch," he suggested.

"Good idea," replied Karar, and they proceeded, uncloaked, into the crowd until they found a spot fifteen feet from the arena. Getting used to people staring at him, Kyriac disregarded Arcadius's stare following him through the crowd, but it lingered in the back of his mind.

"Welcome everyone," started the announcer who stood in the middle of the five hundred foot diameter circular arena in the middle of the stadium, "to the annual mixed martial arts fighting tournament. Once inside the arena, anything goes. However, no weapons are allowed. The winner is declared when the opponent surrenders, leaves the crystal arena, goes unconscious, or in the unfortunate case, dies. Those are the rules. Let the tournament begin!" The announcer left the arena, and all of the lights in the stadium went dark. The announcer started up again, "In the first match of round one, we have the revered Extonic," A spotlight focused on one side of the arena, and Extonic walked through. He couldn't hear the deafening cheers of the crowd around him because the arena was built to silence the outside activity, allowing the fighters to engage in undistracted combat. "Versus the walk-on qualifier Arcadius!" Another spotlight focused on the other side of the arena where Arcadius walked in. Then all of the lights in the arena turned on, but the audience remained in darkness. "Let the fighting begin!" the announcer cheered wildly.

Filled with adrenaline, Extonic started off by running towards Arcadius, imagining how he would tear him apart, but Arcadius remained still as a frozen lake. When Extonic was ten feet away, he bounded for Arcadius, heading straight for the neck. When Extonic was close enough, Arcadius grabbed his right arm and spun around as if to throw him, but stopped suddenly causing Extonic's shoulder to dislocate.

The 'pop' and following groan echoed through the stadium. Many onlookers had to look away.

Extonic knelt down trying to suppress the pain, and Arcadius made no advance towards him. After a few seconds, Extonic bolted upward and swung his other arm at Arcadius's face; Arcadius leaned back to dodge, used Extonic's spinning momentum, and kicked in Extonic's right knee, breaking it and causing him to spin violently downward towards the painfully solid ground.

Despite the pain, Extonic would not give up, so he stood up letting the anger and pain rush through him as the dust from his clothes settle to the ground. Extonic, with his weight on his left leg sized up Arcadius anticipating any future attack. Deciding that he wouldn't, Extonic reached his right shoulder with his good arm. With a smirk on his face and pain running through his entire body, Extonic reset his shoulder into place. The audience cringed.

Able to move his right arm again, Extonic swung it towards Arcadius; Arcadius grabbed his hand, but this time, Extonic knew this was coming and swung his other arm towards Arcadius's occupied arm. At the last second, Arcadius moved Extonic's arm into the path of his own attack, causing Extonic to break his own arm.

Extonic cried out in agony and frustration and tried frantically with his left arm to hit Arcadius. Arcadius deflected Extonic's arm outward, spinning Extonic on his one leg, and before Extonic could pivot back, he punched, with great force, the back of Extonic's neck. Extonic fell, broken neck and unconscious, face-first onto the floor.

Cursing under his breath, SilverX sauntered away to go prepare for his own match.

"Arcadius is the winner!" cheered the announcer while doctors rushed into the arena to carry away Extonic. Arcadius didn't care about this win and showed it as he walked silently out of the arena through the door from which he had entered.

In the following three rounds, Ma had no trouble beating down Marx, Dice quickly dispatched Eddy Nogly, and Bounid defeated Torus.

"In match five," started the announcer, "the match up was Aqua versus Angel. However, Aqua did not show up today, so Angel will automatically qualify for the second round. Now, in the sixth match, we have Shocon, member of Ya's personal guard, versus Shansui, another member of Ya's personal guard." Both fighters entered the arena. "Let the fight begin!"

Both Shocon and Shansui walked towards the middle, bowed to each other, and Shansui said, "I surrender."

"Shocon is the winner," indicated the announcer, noticeably disappointed with that match.

In the next round, Sinerias, being a member of the Empire's army, had an easy fight against Rathenal, and in the eighth match, SilverX knew Marshall Winest as a close friend. With a nod from Marshall, SilverX quickly knocked him out.

"SilverX is the winner!" applauded the announcer. "That is the end of the first round. We will continue with the second round at twelve' o'clock, noon." With that said, the stadium flooded with light once again.

Back at SilverX's base, Dariah waited patiently for the military to mobilize. He knew that the tournament was still in the first round and he had twelve more hours, at least, before the military would start their attack, so he waited, thinking about what he would do.

At Jev's mansion, Jev, Ya, and a handful of soldiers awaited the invasion they assumed inevitable, the same invasion Dariah was trying to stop.

In between rounds at the tournament, the audience cleared out and the grounds crew cleaned out the stadium. People were required to pay separate entrance fees for each round. Kyriac and Karar, however, turned their cloak fields on and stayed in the stadium until the next round. They hid on some rafters so that the cleaning people wouldn't bump into them. Through the boring hours, both of them fell asleep. They awoke as thousands of people poured into their section of the stadium. Climbing down, they uncloaked and returned to their spot.

"Welcome to round two of the tournament!" cheered the all-too-cheerful announcer. "We have four exciting matches to watch. The remaining fighters are Arcadius, Ma, Dice, Bounid, Angel, Shocon, Sinerias, and SilverX." As the announcer's voice stopped, the lights went out. He continued, "in the first match of round two, we have Arcadius versus Ma." A spotlight found Ma standing on the other end of the arena looking slightly friendlier than Arcadius, but not by much. Neither of the fighters looked as though they wanted to fight. "This should be a good match. Let the fight begin!"

Ma started strolling towards Arcadius, and he purposely made his walk appear leisurely to provoke Arcadius to come after him, but Arcadius remained where he was. Since they started five hundred feet apart, the crowd was very displeased by their lack of hustle. After a long walk, Ma was within thirty feet of Arcadius. He bounced back and forth to see how Arcadius followed his movements. Suddenly, he bolted into a sprint. When he was five feet away, he slid trying to trip Arcadius, but Arcadius kicked Ma's foot to the side and cracked his neck when his head arrived in Arcadius's crotch. Ma fell over with no sign of pain before he had gone unconscious, or died.

The entire stadium was ghostly silent for at least five seconds before the announcer broke the silence. "The winner is Arcadius," he said. "For the next match, we have Dice versus Bounid, two very young, very skilled fighters in their first appearance in the annual fighting championship" With a signal from the doctors, he added, "Ma is going to be alright."

Dice and Bounid, though full of youthful energy, lacked experience so much that their match ended up resorting to wrestling. After a long, and very uneventful, fight, Dice finally wore out enough that Bounid could put him into a strangle hold until he passed out.

"The winner is Bounid," said the announcer, cheering more for the fact that the match was over than the outcome. "Next match, we have the walk-on and automatically advanced Angel versus the highly ranked member of Ya's personal guard, Shocon. Let the fight begin!"

Both fighters charged each other at full speed, looking only at the other trying to determine how to defeat him.

"Come on, old man. I am the angel of death, ready to take you away," whispered Angel, though even a whisper was amplified so that everyone, including Shocon, could hear it.

They reached each other; They both dashed off to their right side and turned to attack the other, but Angel was faster. When Shocon turned to face him, he wasn't there. Angel had leaped seven feet into the air and dove behind Shocon headfirst. On his way down he punched Shocon on both sides of his ribs at the same time, leaving Shocon in immense pain and unable to breathe. Angel tucked and rolled out of his dive, spun around and cracked Shocon on the side of his face with his left hand. Shocon was knocked unconscious.

"Whose god is true now?" smirked Angel to Shocon's motionless body.

"The winner is Angel," exclaimed the announcer. Walk-on combatants historically never won, so to have two walk-ons make it this far was a momentous moment for the tournament. The announcer was sharing his enthusiasm for the remarkable event through his noticeable favoritism for Angel and Arcadius. "The final match of round two consists of Sinerias, a member of the empire's army, versus council member SilverX," stated the announcer. "Let the fight begin."

These two warriors fought with honor; they had both been in many tournaments and wanted to see traditions upheld. They jogged to the middle where they bowed to each other, and with a nod, Sinerias threw his hand towards SilverX. Without hesitation, SilverX punched Sinerias's oncoming fist with the intent to show his strength and invulnerability to pain. As well trained as he was, Sinerias made sure to show no sign of pain; instead, he opened the palm of his hand using his broken hand to chop and parry. SilverX made sure to not give him enough time to recover from the last hit, so he swept his left foot from right to left to trip Sinerias. Sinerias saw it coming and kicked SilverX's other leg. SilverX lost his balance, but he grabbed Sinerias at the shoulder. He rolled backward and threw Sinerias with his legs. Then, he quickly kipped to his feet, flipped backward, and landed with his knee on Sinerias's throat.

"Surrender," Sinerias choked out, and SilverX immediately got to his feet and helped Sinerias to his.

"The winner is SilverX!" commended the announcer. "That concludes round two. Round three will start at six 'o' clock tonight."

During this break, Karar felt like leaving to go eat. When she mentioned this to Kyriac, he was reminded abruptly that his stomach existed, and it told him that it was empty; he readily agreed to leave.

As Kyriac and Karar exited, there were surprisingly few people nearby after hundreds of thousands of people had packed themselves into that stadium. They all dispersed to carry on with their busy lives between rounds. After getting lunch, the two of them walked around the city for several hours. All the while, Karar tried to think of something to say to start a conversation, but never did. She kept thinking her words would sound too stupid, or would annoy Kyriac, and her nervousness accelerated. Kyriac, too, was trying to think of something to say. Physically, he was seventeen, but socially, he was thirteen. He liked Karar, but didn't know how to show it. He tried, with every bit of his power, to make sure everything he did was good enough for her, which only caused him to become clumsy and full of jitters. So, for several hours, they walked around, clumsy and nervous, both thinking of the other, wishing they'd say something, anything to break this uncomfortable silence, but neither did.

They arrived back at the stadium just before it opened again for observers, so they cloaked and went into the stadium; meeting at the spot they had before.

"Welcome to round three of the tournament!" cheered the announcer. "For our first fight, we will have unbreakable Arcadius versus the young and powerful Bounid." As before, the spotlights focused on the two fighters as the rest of the stadium went dark. "Two walk-ons made it this far in the tournament folks. This should be an exciting match! Let the fight begin!"

Bounid jogged across the arena to meet Arcadius. At full sprint, he threw his right fist towards Arcadius's face. When Bounid reached the point of being off-balance, Arcadius slid over towards his own right and struck Bounid's back with his left arm, pushing him to the ground. Bounid bolted back to his feet and advanced towards Arcadius again and tried to punch him with his right fist. Arcadius grabbed Bounid's oncoming hand with his left hand, twisted it back, breaking it, and sent his right palm into Bounid's face, breaking Bounid's nose. As his hand hit Bounid's face, Arcadius released Bounid's hand, and Bounid flew backwards landing on his back. Despite the pain, Bounid was not unconscious. Bounid surrendered, knowing he could not defeat Arcadius.

"The winner is Arcadius!" the announcer cheered. Showing no emotion, Arcadius exited the arena. "Next match, we have Angel versus SilverX. Let the fight begin!"

Angel recognized SilverX's desire to keep tradition and shake hands in the middle, but he had no intention of fighting fair. He started jogging out towards the middle, and so did SilverX. They met in the middle, and SilverX held out his hand. Angel grabbed SilverX's hand, pulled SilverX towards him while sending his other hand towards SilverX's face. SilverX expected Angel to do something like this, so he ducked to avoid Angel's fist and wrapped his other hand around Angel's legs, picked him up, and threw him into the air. When Angel was just above SilverX's head on the way back down, SilverX crouched, jumped, and put his right fist into Angel's face spinning him around and making him land on his back. Not giving Angel a chance to regain his composure, SilverX leaped over to him, put his knees on his arms and choked him until he passed out.

"The winner is SilverX! SilverX advances to the final round against Arcadius at midnight tonight," praised the announcer.

During this break, Kyriac and Karar once again walked around silently, ate again, and returned to the stadium just before it opened up. Like before, they both were so nervous, they couldn't even see how anxious the other was acting.

"Welcome to the final round! This is an exciting match up. We have Arcadius, who is fighting in his very first tournament, against SilverX, the favorite coming into this tournament. This fight decides the world's strongest. Let the final round begin!" the announcer shouted as enthusiastically as he could muster.

SilverX still had no idea how he would beat Arcadius, so he started walking slowly and deliberately across the arena towards Arcadius to provide himself time to think and monitor how Arcadius reacts; Arcadius remained unwavering.

As SilverX walked, his army started to mobilize towards the capital city, Multrop, from the Siberian city Daskard, but standing in their way was the weaponless silhouette of Dariah.

"Come on!" cried SilverX as he charged Arcadius. "Fight me!"

"Come on!" cried Dariah, "I'll fight you all."

SilverX lunged towards Arcadius, who grabbed SilverX's leading arm and swung him around behind him like he had before, but as SilverX was being tossed, he swung his leg towards Arcadius's stomach. Arcadius flipped over SilverX's leg, twisting SilverX's arm around causing him to spin in air and slam into the ground. Arcadius, still holding SilverX's arm, put his foot on SilverX's neck and popped the shoulder out of place.

"I will take on each and every one of you if I have to," Dariah shouted towards the army facing him. A few chuckled, but more feared the confident Dariah. All of the soldiers knew he was strong, but none of them knew to what extent Dariah's power was. They knew SilverX feared him, so they feared him more.

Before SilverX could react to the tremendous pain in his shoulder, Arcadius jolted him up by his dislocated arm and swung him around so he faced Arcadius. As he did so, he swung his other arm, the one not holding SilverX, towards SilverX's bad shoulder.

"And every soldier who tries to fight me, I will not only kill, but I will find your family, and I will kill them too."

SilverX frantically threw his good fist at Arcadius's face. Arcadius stopped the fist with his hand and crushed it with ease. SilverX cried out in pain for the first time. Wanting to prove his point, Arcadius pulled on SilverX's bad arm, popping it back into place and then kicked, with both legs, SilverX's chest dislocating both arms.

"I will burn down your houses, and laugh at the screams of the children

I left inside. And when I am through with your house, I will burn down the entire village laughing your name so they know who caused this; they will know that you are to blame for their deaths." Dariah's laugh was so menacing that many of the soldiers shivered in fear as though the devil stood before them. Many had already left, yet far too many remained. His voice chilled them, darkening their vision, so they feel all alone.

Arcadius, not done, grabbed SilverX by the throat and threw him against the arena wall. SilverX hit the wall six feet above the ground, and before gravity completed its job, Arcadius dove into him and slammed him against the wall a second time. Arcadius backed away to reveal a small crack in the crystalline wall and SilverX lying, still conscious on the ground, struggling to breathe and attempting to stand up.

"I will give you one chance to run away before I kill you, and when I kill you, I will do it slowly and as painfully as possible. In fact, I will kill you with your own limbs ripped from your bodies as you struggle helplessly. I bet your blood tastes sweet in this cold." It was as though even his breath was menacing. Steam rose from his skin as his words chilled the army's bones.

After a few minutes, SilverX was able to stand up, and, using the wall for support, he relocated his shoulders. Then he tore a piece from his clothing and tied up his wrist.

"Are you ready?" asked Arcadius.

"Those who fight deserve to die!" screamed Dariah.

"Humph," grunted SilverX.

"Well then, let's hope you provide more sport this time," laughed Arcadius.

SilverX charged Arcadius, but when he was close enough, Arcadius slid to his right side and pushed him to the ground. SilverX immediately got up, but Arcadius hit him on the shoulder back to the ground. SilverX got up a third time just to be knocked down again.

"Alright bring it on! I can tell the rest of you want to die!" Almost all of the soldiers had left and the remaining few looked around at one another confused and scared. Dariah started to charge those who remained, and all of them began to run away. "You guys can fight, can't you? Get back here!" he cried out after them, but they were all gone.

SilverX was furious. He couldn't even get to Arcadius let alone hit him. His anger was rising and he kept moving faster and less controlled. Each time he tried to attack Arcadius; he'd get knocked back down. Finally, SilverX became so infuriated the air around him heated rapidly, and the crowd could see a mirage of heat on him, like the heat one would see on the horizon in the desert. SilverX darted up while swinging his fist at Arcadius's stomach, much faster than he had ever done before. It connected, knocking the wind out of Arcadius; then SilverX sent another punch, this time at Arcadius's face. It connected too, sending Arcadius flying back ten feet, but SilverX wasn't done. He dove into the air, ready to crush Arcadius's throat with his knee. Right before he landed, Arcadius grabbed his leading knee, swung him around, into the ground, pushed himself up, and threw SilverX along the ground into the wall again.

When SilverX stood up, the heat around him had vanished, and his energy had gone with it. Arcadius stood twenty feet from him, laughing. It was a very quiet laugh, but it was still a laugh.

"What? What's so funny?" demanded SilverX.

"I wanted to see how powerful you are, and that was it. Ha, you hit me twice."

"What?" SilverX didn't understand.

"It's time for a real fight now. Your time is up." Arcadius instantly had silvery-clear waves about him as he darted towards SilverX. SilverX tried to block the oncoming attack, but he went through the block as if it wasn't there. One punch to the chest sent SilverX flying through the barrier of the arena wall. SilverX was eliminated for exiting the arena.

"We have a winner!" the announcer was excited beyond belief. "Arcadius wins!" The crowd had mixed emotions. Some were booing, others cheering wildly. "Do you have anything to say?" the announcer asked as SilverX struggled up, scowling greatly.

"I want to fight *Kyriac*."

Chapter 16

The crowd's commotion changed to whispers.

"Kyriac is a criminal on the run, he is not here," shared the announcer. "Regardless, why would you want to face him, you've proven you're the strongest man in the world."

"I believe Kyriac is stronger than any of these competitors, and he is here." As he spoke, he pointed a finger straight at Kyriac. Those around Kyriac quickly dashed away, except Karar. With one hand wrapped in Kyriac's and the other grasping tightly to a sola gun, Karar stood firm, ready to fight for Kyriac if needed. Kyriac knew Karar was there, he felt her hand in his, but still he stared straight at this champion who called out his name in a challenge.

Thirty arena guards rushed to surround the two of them. Nobody was permitted to bring guns of any sort into the tournament, including guards, so these guards were equipped with probes that stunned assailants.

"Get on the ground!" commanded a guard.

"If you do not comply we will be forced to hurt you!" shouted another.

Kyriac did not move, nor did his eyes deviate from Arcadius.

"Get on the ground!" commanded the guard again with more force. "You have five seconds before we take you down!"

Neither Kyriac nor Karar moved.

"Four!" barked the guard.

"*What does Arcadius want from me?*" thought Kyriac.

"Three!"

"*Why'd he do this?*" he thought

Just as the soldier said "two," Karar let go of Kyriac's hand, grabbed her other sola, pointed them straight outward from her arms, and said, "Anyone who comes closer, dies."

"She's got sola guns!" cried a guard.

"Hold your ground," ordered the one who had been counting, obviously the commander of the group. He continued, "Karar Alumin, A.K.A. Pilot Raider, you are under arrest by order of the Earth's Empire. Kyriac, you are under arrest for the murder of the Guardian."

With a flick of the commander's wrist, the rest of the guards began to close the fifty-foot gap. Karar fired ten shots, five from each sola. Each shot was aimed at a different guard, and each shot drained their shields entirely.

"I'll keep shooting unless you back away," warned Karar.

"That's not possible," cried the commander.

"It's possible now," smirked Karar.

Fearing death, the commander led his troops away as disheveled as ants in a flood. With a clear path to the arena, Kyriac began walking towards Arcadius.

Though the tournament was over, the stadium was hardly empty. There were still a lot of people still in support of Kyriac despite the slander in the news. Most people couldn't get a television or access to the news in any way, so the slander moved slower than the stories about Kyriac. It was very hard to tarnish his name with the world in the state it was in.

Kyriac and Arcadius positioned themselves so there was fifty feet between them.

A moment passed where both warriors stood and looked at the other as if they were waiting for a sign to start. Then, with a nod from Arcadius, Kyriac and Arcadius started sprinting towards each other. Within a couple of seconds, they were five feet apart. Arcadius bolted right and Kyriac went to his own left. Because they were going so fast, they bolted diagonally towards each other. Kyriac crouched and swept his right leg around his back trying to knock Arcadius down. Arcadius jumped into the air led by his left leg. When he was above Kyriac, he swung his right leg forward as hard as he could into Kyriac's face.

Despite the discomfort, Kyriac was able to brace himself from falling over with his arms. Arcadius landed, spun around, and lunged again at Kyriac, this time kicking him in the back of the head. Kyriac tumbled forward, rolled back up to his feet, and turned around to face Arcadius; however, Arcadius was already there, throwing a fist at Kyriac's face. Kyriac ducked, and tried to punch Arcadius in the stomach, but Arcadius rolled to his right, grabbed Kyriac's arm, and kicked Kyriac's upper chest, just next to the shoulder shattering the joint. Kyriac focused his mind to suppress the pain. Frantically, Kyriac swung his other arm down onto Arcadius's knee. Arcadius wasn't fast enough to move away from Kyriac's desperate attempt, and his leg bent backwards breaking the knee. Kyriac then swung his leg around and tripped Arcadius. Arcadius fell backwards. Kyriac leaped forward towards Arcadius to land with his knee, but Arcadius kicked Kyriac away with his non-broken leg.

They both immediately stood up at looked at each other.

"I am impressed," admitted Arcadius.

Kyriac said nothing; he just stood catching his breath.

"You are very powerful. That kind of power can tear a man apart. Let me show you." Arcadius focused his energy between his hands. Shortly, a plasma-like substance grew out of the middle. Kyriac focused his own energy trying to replicate what Arcadius had done. Before he could create the plasma, Arcadius threw his at Kyriac. Afraid, Kyriac raised his hand up to block. The energy dispersed on Kyriac's hand, singeing only his arms.

"I had no idea you knew how to do that. I am sorry for underestimating you. What else do you know?"

"I can create heat like that," replied Kyriac. "That's all. Is that all you're doing?"

"Try this." Arcadius held his hands out in front of him a couple inches wider than his shoulders. In between his hands, he focused his energy and ten seconds later there was a ball of flaming, crackling, energy hovering in front of him.

"It takes an extreme amount of energy to create, but because of the high energy, you can move it around by focusing your energy from there, as long as you never lose focus on it. I suppose it's like telepathy or something, but I've never been able to control two; as soon as I make the second I lose focus on the first and it fades away," explained Arcadius in an excited tone. "If you ever figure out how to create two, please let me know. Oh yeah, I call it an orb. Try it."

Kyriac tried lifting his right arm but could not anymore.

"I cannot, but I will," assured Kyriac.

"Fair enough. It was a pleasure fighting you, but I must go. I hope we will meet again," said Arcadius as he activated his cloak field and disappeared.

As he relaxed, Kyriac began to feel the pain rush from his shoulder. When he looked over to see the damage, Karar was by his side.

"We must leave as well," she said, and they turned on their cloak generators and snuck away to their vehicle stored three miles away.

Chapter 17

Back at the Guardian's mansion, Jev had doctors to help take care of Kyriac. The nanites were too slow and inaccurate to fix a shattered joint such as this one.

"Dariah told the truth, Arcadius beat SilverX," Karar explained to Jev.

"Yes, I know, I saw the match on the news, and I saw Kyriac's match too. It seems Kyriac has made an impression in Amena and the Mascien systems. Arcadius as you probably know is a Mascien." Karar nodded. "It would appear the only reason he would risk being here on earth is because he missed Kyriac when you two were in Amena," explained Jev. Since well before the unification, Masciens were banned from the Earth Empire by Crotonee due to the general disregard for most of his policies.

"So, he's just a fan of Kyriac's?" pondered Karar out loud.

"See, the Masciens, as individuals, are much stronger than humans, so from an evolutionary standpoint, they are superior. I believe that Arcadius wanted to test his superiority over the human race by defeating Kyriac, our apparent furthest evolved human. I also believe many Masciens feel the same way as Arcadius, but there are those who see Kyriac as their link to the past. They used to be so incredibly similar to us, but that was thousands of years ago. Unless you're looking closely, they still do actually. He's the gap, though, between Masciens and humans. This is why they are so obsessed with him."

"I understand," stated Karar. "Kyriac is the midpoint of Mascien and human evolution, so he's at the point where, historically, Masciens were evolving the most. If I understand Mascien history right, what you're saying is that Kyriac is going to be stronger than all Masciens and humans."

"Except Ricoba, who is just like Kyriac, only centuries older," recognized Jev, and then added, "and he's as smart as a human too. With the potential he possesses, it's no wonder everyone expects him to save them."

"No one can beat me; no one!" cried Angel from the top of Sil Tower in Moscow, Russia. "SilverX, you will see my power. Watch me unleash it. You are nothing but evil, and those who don't see this must die. This entire city must die."

Since Sil Marxiq's father was banished to Russia, the Marxiq family had slowly gained power in Russia, until Sil Marxiq was 18 years old, when he formed a revolt upon his father and created a people's nation ruled by Sil Marxiq. Russia, under the control of Sil, became a very powerful and economically stable country, despite the taxation from Crotonee. The people worshiped Sil Marxiq as a leader and a leader in the church, and when the unification came, the people unanimously stood by as Sil tried to defend Russia from Crotonee's powerful military. As history tells, Sil Marxiq failed to defend his country, but his country came forward to defend him; Sil was never caught or killed, and the Empire didn't pursue him because they had too many other things to worry about. After the war was over, he gave himself the alias SilverX out of disgrace. Until he freed his people from the tyrannical empire, he could not bring himself to be called Sil again because his people loved that person too much to be let down by him. Even after the unification, those in Moscow still supported and worshiped Sil Marxiq, and Sil tower was 145-story tower in the center of the city. In the very top of the tower, there was a cathedral, in which Sil used to preach, and on top of that cathedral, Angel stood looking over the entire city with hatred in his soul.

"I am the angel of death, ready to take you all away!" cried Angel as he dropped from the top of the tower. He plummeted fifty stories before opening his wings and igniting his rocket pack. Still flying downward, he tilted his back upward and arced his flight so he was flying parallel to the ground three feet above the desolate street. When he was a safe distance away, Angel pressed a button on his wrist. A series of explosions triggered in the base of Sil Tower, causing it to collapse; one hundred and forty-four stories fell to the ground in the middle of Moscow. Nearby buildings, ravaged by flying debris, crumbled to the ground as well. When the dust settled, Sil Tower and all buildings within a half-mile were gone. All those within those towers were dead. Over two million people died in Angel's attack with a plague of panic inflicting those still alive.

"Sorry to interrupt," intruded Ya as Karar, Kyriac, and Jev were eating dinner, only hours after Kyriac was done being operated on. "SilverX wishes to speak with Kyriac."

"Why?" inquired Karar.

"He brought no weapons or military. He said there is something he needs to talk about with Kyriac, but he won't tell anyone else."

"Tell him no," responded Jev.

"He also said that you all may be present to hear what he has to say. He seems frantic. I've never seen him like this," continued Ya.

"Why would SilverX show up here after his loss at the tournament, and his army was averted?" inquired Karar.

"It must be important," added Jev.

"Let him in," commanded Kyriac, saying the first thing since dinner had begun.

"Are you sure, Kyriac? Your shoulder isn't fully healed yet," asked Jev. "You two have fought the last two times you've seen each other."

"I am," replied Kyriac.

"Let him in then," commanded Jev.

Ya left the dining room, and two minutes later entered again with SilverX. SilverX, despite his change of clothing and nanites working on his body, still looked beat up from the fight the previous night. SilverX sat down and appeared to search for the words he was about to share.

"Kyriac," he began. "This is hard for me right now, but I need your help. One of those walk-ons from the tournament, Angel he called himself, has committed a heinous act against my people. Moscow is in ruins and there has to be over two million people dead because of him. I realized now, that I have become greedy in my endeavors and I've lost sight of the reason I tried to gain power. Now those people who depended on me, those who trusted me to bring them a powerful nation; they are dead." SilverX laid his head down in his arms. Ten seconds passed and he started again. "I've sent members of my guard out to try and find him, but it's obvious that Angel is far too powerful for any of them. I need your help, Kyriac, to help bring him to justice."

"Why do you need me? All you've done so far is try to kill me. I have my own problems, and you're the cause of them."

"If you help me, I assure you the Council will stop pursuing you."

"I will only help you, if you pardon Karar and me," insisted Kyriac. "And Jev must be recognized as Guardian and give the authority he is owed."

"Absolutely, you have my support for those things," agreed SilverX.

"And, know this isn't a favor for you. This is because there is a murderer out there."

"Thank you, Kyriac. I will be forever grateful of your kindness. If you ever need anything, please let me know. I am in your debt."

"Kyriac, your shoulder isn't healed. I don't think you should be doing this," warned Jev.

"I'm fine," assured Kyriac as he pulled his arm from his sling. "See, I can move it fine."

"Amazing," thought Karar. *"I think Jev is right about his evolution."* Jev's expression was beyond shock, but he had no words to match.

"If any of my men find Angel before you, you will be sent the coordinates. Thank you once again for your aid. I must be leaving. Obviously, I have so much I need to do," SilverX said as he turned around and left.

Chapter 18

"Excuse me," called out Angel, but the man kept walking. "Sir!" he tried louder.

The man continued walking as if the shouts weren't directed towards him, though there was no one else around this barren part of what used to be Atlanta, Georgia.

"Ex, is that you?" shouted Angel, but was ignored. The man was traveling at a brisk pace, so much that Angel had to jog to catch up. Looking closely at the man he had caught up to, he continued, "it is you. Why are you in my neighborhood?"

The man stared blankly at Angel.

"You know me, from the tournament. I'm Angel."

"No," simply stated the man.

"What do you mean, no? I fought in the tournament; I beat Shocon. I was unrated going into the tournament and made it to the second round," boasted Angel.

"I don't know anything about what you just said; in fact I don't know much of anything shy the last few days or so," admitted the man.

"*That's why he's been missing* thought Angel. *SilverX must've wiped his brain and dumped him in America after that defeat in the tournament. Fortunately for both of us, he wound up in my territory. If SilverX doesn't want him, I'll take him.*" "Listen," said Angel, "I know you better than most anyone."

"So you say," interjected the man.

"You are Extonic Jarod. You were, at one point, employed as the second hand man to a man named Sil Marxiq, or SilverX as most of the world knows him. SilverX, after losing the tournament three days ago, obviously decided to use you as the scapegoat, and he brainwashed you and dumped you off here in America, the world's most desolate junkyard as an example to his people of what happens when they fail him."

"Oh... why would he do that?" Ex asked sarcastically, partially to humor Angel, with an inkling of interest rising up. Having no knowledge of oneself is frightening, no memory at all is worse. Here, Extonic didn't know what to think, or who to trust, but he was willing to take any opportunity to regain the memory he had lost.

"Listen, what I'm telling you is the truth; the only reason I'm telling you this is because SilverX is now both of our enemies."

"If what you're saying is the truth, then why'd you call out my name?" he challenged skeptically.

"It was only a hunch, up until you verified it."

"Well then, why wouldn't this SilverX just kill me?"

"Because he wants you to suffer. He... he's done this before to people; he erases their memory and drops them off in America where they have to fend for themselves without knowing who they are. He knows people can't survive very long here. It's his form of punishment."

"I can see what I would have against him; what do you have against him?" asked Extonic, and then added, "you seem to know who you are."

"This is a longer story," he began. "SilverX's father used to be the leader of Morocco, but foolishly tried to invade Algeria. When he failed, he was banished to Siberia, where he ruled for years. SilverX led a coup d'état against his father justifying his actions with the slow economic growth. It is true that SilverX made Russia one of the most powerful nations before the unification, but he did so by ruling with fear. If anyone failed to do their part in his society, they would be tortured. My family was subject to that torture. During the tournament, he tried to take over Earth, but his army was held back by Dariah, the only person they fear more than SilverX. He is now desperate to take over because all his attempts recently have failed and he is losing power over his people. With your help, we can, we can actually stop him, despite his strength and military. Together, you and I can stop him."

"Why me?"

"Because you are Extonic, the Executioner, one of the strongest persons on the planet. You and I complement each other. Together, we have the strength to beat SilverX. I need your help Extonic, I need your help. We're the only ones who can stop him, and the world needs us to. Please come with me. I can explain everything after we do this, and maybe SilverX somehow saved your memory, but we have to stop him; he's going to try something really desperate soon."

"I don't know what to think. You seem to know me well; better than I know myself. If what you're saying is true, then I have to go with you, and I have to stop SilverX. If he did this to me, what's he going to do to the rest of the world? He sounds like a very sick person who must be stopped. I'll go with you, but you have to promise you'll help me get my memory."

"Of course, you have my word."

"Sir, we can use Cyber Dariah to kill Angel as well as Dariah. It is a very simple program, unlike Beronith, so it's relatively easy to add in another target," suggested one of SilverX's scientists.

"That sounds like a good idea," agreed SilverX, "do it." he added. The soldier acknowledged and indicated it would take another half hour.

"I'll stay," SilverX said firmly.

After the half-hour, the scientist turned to find SilverX impatiently waiting the same spot as before.

"Well?" asked SilverX.

"Yes, he's pretty much done. You'll be able to release him once he's fully booted up," replied the scientist.

"Then do it," said SilverX.

"Of course," replied the scientist as he opened a door, three feet away from SilverX. A robot that resembled Dariah, almost perfectly, proceeded to walk out. There were noticeable qualities that appeared inhuman. His movements were harsh and sudden, his eyes did not blink, he didn't breathe, and he didn't make any normal human motions at all. "Don't worry," the scientist assured, "we've put much more work into Cyber Beronith; he will be flawless. This one is just for the tasks at hand and then we'll dispose of him; after all, you said we only need one cyber."

"He had better perform. Dariah, what are your orders?" demanded SilverX.

"Kill Angel and Dariah," replied Cyber Dariah.

Walking out of the room, SilverX ordered, "release him from this base."

"Of course, sir," mumbled the scientist, too late for SilverX to hear.

Chapter 19

Upon leaving the laboratory, SilverX saw his lead assistant, Edward, running towards him.

"He's here! Angel is here!" bellowed Edward.

"How could he find me? Let Kyriac know," demanded SilverX. Amidst the cursing that followed, he added, "have him meet Angel outside. I'll lure him out."

"We need you here, Kyriac," said the voice from Kyriac's communication receiver that SilverX had given to him. "These are the coordinates. Please hurry, SilverX is trying to hold them off. I have to go, we're counting on you." The receiver went dark except the coordinates sent.

"Kyriac," began Jev in a low calm voice, such a voice that would imply that something very serious was going on. "Before you go, I need to tell you something. It cannot wait, you must know this. The world might be about to change dramatically, and you are at the center of it all."

"What are you trying to tell me?" asked Kyriac, now worried about what Jev might say.

"You aren't who everyone thinks you are; however you are abnormal. The human race has remained primarily the same for thousands of years, and just recently you and probably a dozen other people have become extremely strong, human wise that is. As you may know, the Mascien race is evolved further beyond us, but only because of one Mascien, Ricoba. You are like Ricoba. There are others. SilverX and Angel are strong, but none of them are like you. In only a few weeks, you've grown stronger both physically and mentally. These other people have trained their entire lives to become what they are now. Now, like I said, you aren't what the people of earth think you are. They all think you are the savior, someone who will make everything right, but you must remember, you are still human. You can die like the rest of us, but if you die, the hopes and dreams of billions of people die with you. I guess what I'm trying to say is, you're more important to everyone if you're alive. Be careful who you choose to support Kyriac because there are those who will use you like Ice did and Ritwo, and like SilverX tries to. Your life will change this world, and I hope it is for the better. This said, your life is your own; I will arrange that you are provided your own home somewhere secluded, so you are not bothered, and you may choose how you live your life from now on. I will, of course, always be here if you need me."

Kyriac walked away from Jev with all of what Jev had said dashing through his mind. Many things were answered, but at the same time many more questions originated.

"Angel," spoke SilverX's voice through the intercom system, "if you want me, meet me on the surface. These halls are no place for a fight. Perhaps we could to talk this over."

"Sounds like a trap," muttered Angel unaware that SilverX could hear him.

"I assure you, this is not a trap. I'm the one you want, and I'm letting you know that I'm waiting on the surface. Come fight me; leave the rest of these people alone."

"I'll fight you, but be warned, if this is a trap, everyone here will die here today, on that, you have my word."

Without further questioning each other's intent, SilverX and Angel proceeded to the surface. SilverX arrived first and waited three minutes for Angel to arrive.

"I must say, I am surprised this isn't a trap," informed Angel

"I beat you in the tournament, why would I need tricks to beat you here?" boasted SilverX.

"Because," laughed Angel, "I wasn't planning on playing fair." As he said this, Extonic appeared from the door Angel had come from. He was holding two spears, and he handed one to Angel. "I found him lost in

America where I presume you dumped him after you erased his memory as you tried to do mine."

"What?" responded both SilverX and Extonic simultaneously.

"That's right, I was once your patsy too, but as soon as I learned what our schemes really amounted to, I wanted out; however you had other plans for me. You erased my memory, dumped me in America, and framed me for the murders of eight council members. What you didn't know was that I saved my memory and gave it to an associate of mine, and here I am today with another of your patsies ready to stop you once and for all," explained Angel.

"Bathlis, huh?" guessed SilverX, "You should know, before you die, you did kill those councilmen. You were convinced they were working for me, and you thought I had the world corrupted. You had lost your mind to the grips of paranoia, and I didn't erase your memory. For two years, you grew worse in a mental institution, so they wiped your mind. I'm not sure how you ended up in America. You really should've been in prison."

"Lies!" cried Angel as he rushed towards SilverX. SilverX dodged to the right as Angel plunged his spear forward. Before Angel could regain his composure and strike again, SilverX kicked the backs of his knees and grabbed both Angel's neck and his spear. He tossed the spear aside and slammed Angel backward into the dirt. Losing no time, SilverX swung his open hand towards Angel's face, but Angel punched SilverX in the face first causing him to miss Angel. Angel scrambled to his feet and backed up several feet away from SilverX.

"What are you doing, Extonic, help me," demanded Angel "We must stop him." Extonic remained still, thinking about SilverX's story about Angel. "Don't let him fool you; he must be stopped. Would I bring you here to find out I've been lying to you?" Extonic was convinced. He nodded and walked over near Angel.

Simultaneously, both fighter's tensed their muscles, ready to pounce on SilverX, but as they did so, a helicopter appeared over top of a hill five hundred feet away.

"Perfect timing," whispered SilverX.

"What is this?" demanded Angel as he pulled out a detonator.

"Put away the detonator, Angel; It won't work anyway," requested SilverX. "I've invited a friend. I hope you don't mind" Angel tried the switch anyway, but as SilverX had said, it was no use.

The helicopter landed a few seconds later and Kyriac, Karar, and Dariah emerged from the craft.

Dariah was the first to speak, "please, I urge you all to solve this peacefully. I have seen, first hand, the effects of fighting. If you fight, not all of you will leave here today. Your lives are at stake. Please reconsider, all of you."

SilverX was shocked by the change in Dariah's outlook on fighting, but nonetheless he maintained his vision focused on Angel and Extonic. "Thank you for coming to my aid, Kyriac. Now if you wouldn't mind, could you help me remove these pests?"

"Extonic?" asked Kyriac.

"He's been brainwashed, somehow, by Angel. If you can, don't kill him, but these two must be stopped here today before they kill more people."

"Don't listen to him!" cried Angel. "Everything he says is a lie."

"I know that you killed many people Angel, and for that I cannot forgive you. Whatever transgressions SilverX has committed will catch up with him eventually. This is your time to pay," stated Kyriac with a large amount of new found confidence in his voice. The confidence startled all those present since Kyriac had, in every other public appearance, been so quiet, but the words of Jev gave way to a new mentality.

"This will be your end too, Kyriac. I am the Angel of Death ready to take all of you away," said Angel as he pulled a handful of small pellets. He threw the pellets in the direction of SilverX and Kyriac. Before they reached Kyriac or SilverX, Extonic and Angel bolted towards SilverX. On the way, Angel scooped up his spear. Before the pellets collided with their targets, Kyriac and SilverX flew into the air. Dariah rushed over to Karar, picked her up, and lifted her out of harm's way. Some of the pellets collided with the helicopter and exploded on impact, rendering the helicopter useless and in pieces. Before SilverX landed, both Extonic and Angel threw their spears at him. He deflected Angel's, but Extonic's spear hit him in the right side of his chest. As it connected, so did Angel's foot with SilverX's face.

Angel and Extonic kept their momentum going towards Kyriac. Kyriac landed, hurdled over the tumbling SilverX, and drew both his daggers and his sword. Karar caught the spear that SilverX deflected and she charged towards the two attackers. Kyriac swung his sword towards to oncoming Angel who dove to the ground and rolled behind Kyriac. Extonic reached and grabbed Kyriac's sword carrying hand, and Angel stood up and grabbed the other. They then both punched Kyriac one in his stomach, the other in his back. Both Extonic and Angel drew their arms back to swing again, but Karar plummeted Angel's spear through Angel's spinal cord and heart, killing him instantly with his arm free and a dagger still in it. Kyriac swung his dagger into Extonic's neck, killing him as well.

Dariah rushed to aid SilverX as Karar caught Kyriac as he fell forward. As Karar caught him, Extonic and Angel hit the ground completely lifeless.

"Jev, we need medical aid," Dariah spoke into his receiver and added, "and a helicopter."

"Ya and I are coming," replied Jev, "hang in there." As he was saying this, another helicopter arrived at the scene. Instead of Ya and Jev stepping from the aircraft, out stepped Ma, one of the fighters from the tournament.

"I heard there was trouble, so I came to see what I could do to help," he said. "My name's Ma, I saw four of you at the tournament, and I presume you are Dariah." He pointed towards Dariah, and Dariah nodded.
"I presume I cannot do anything for those two," Ma stated pointing at Extonic and Angel, "how about SilverX, is he going to be okay?"

"Only if we can get medical help soon," informed Dariah.

By this time, Kyriac was able to stand up on his own again, and he pulled his dagger from Extonic's neck. He wiped off his bloody dagger and placed all his weapons back in their sheaths. As his last sword slid into its sheath, Jev and Ya appeared in their aircraft. As Jev stepped out, the first thing he noticed was Extonic and Angel lying dead, but the first thing that Ya noticed was the presence of Ma.

"I'll take him to a hospital and send for another helicopter to pick the rest of you up," volunteered Jev.

As Jev left with SilverX, Ma stated, "I could take one of you with me in my helicopter if you want." Nobody responded, so Ma was about to offer again when another person appeared on the cold landscape only a short distance from them.

Dariah was speechless as he gazed into the seemingly lifeless eyes of a figure that looked almost exactly like him.

"What is this?" inquired Kyriac.

"This is SilverX's doing," Dariah put forward. "I know it."

"Who are you?" demanded Kyriac.

"I am Dariah," said the inhuman voice of the figure standing before them. "Dariah must die." As he said it, he lunged towards Dariah. Dariah dove aside.

"Kyriac, help me," implored Dariah.

"Right," agreed Kyriac as he readied his weapons again. Dariah rushed back towards Kyriac. The robot rushed towards Dariah again, but Kyriac got in his way. With ease, the robot tossed Kyriac aside and continued towards Dariah.

Dariah took the full blow of the robot's fist into his stomach. Without pausing, the robot swung his other arm around into the side of Dariah's head. Kyriac got back up and ran towards the robot. He swung his leg around towards the robot's feet trying to trip him; however, the robot saw this attack coming and lifted his closest leg in anticipation, and when Kyriac's leg arrived, he stomped on the incoming leg.

"Ahh!" Kyriac cried in pain. While the robot continued to put as much pressure as he could in the place where he had just broken Kyriac's leg.

"*You are still human,*" Jev's words echoed through Kyriac's brain. The pain was incredible. The robot grinded his foot around on the broken pieces of Kyriac's leg. After only two seconds of this, Dariah regained his composure and leaped towards the robot only to be punched in the throat as he came within range of the robot's fist. The robot was about to turn back to Kyriac to finish him off when Ma jumped forward. As Ma dove into action, Ya leapt into attack mode as well. Ma punched the robot in its stomach region while Ya spun around back and kicked it in the back. The robot staggered leaving enough time for Ma to jump and kick the robot in the face causing it to fall backward. As it fell, Ya punched it on the side making it flip over while it fell. When it was nearly to the ground, Ma came down on its chest hard with his fist. As his fist fell, Ma felt a new strength brew within him causing his fist to strike down even harder. Upon striking the metal body of a robot, Ma expected pain to shoot through his arm, but none came. He struck again and again until the mental body of this robot gave way leaving the exposed organic circuitry of this being. Ma struck down one last time going all the way through the robot to the other side of the metal shell leaving it lifeless at last.

Standing up, Ma realized that Ya was no longer focused on the body of their opponent, but that of another new figure that had entered the Siberian landscape on which they stood. Seeing no possible way for this figure to get there, Ma found himself puzzled. Also puzzling was the fact that Kyriac was standing next to this figure apparently in no pain whatsoever.

"Ya and Ma, it has been a while," the new figure began. "This world is about to become unsafe for you. In order to preserve our God, you should come back with me to our plane." Instantly a rift opened near the figure, and Ya and Ma obediently walked through the rift as though without a word spoken in opposition.

"Um... Jev," started Kyriac. "We're fine now, but there are only three of us left, Dariah, Karar and I."

"Ya and Ma died," gasped Jev.

"No..." continued Kyriac, struggling deeply to find the appropriate words to describe what he saw. "They left with some other person to another world, I guess. I really don't know what happened. I just really want to leave area before another person shows up."

On the way home, Kyriac found out that Ya and Ma were demigods. Jev worried that upon leaving this world, they were leaving it to become doomed. Whatever was about to happen, the gods had just abandoned Earth to face it alone. This was all they could know for sure.

Chapter 20

SilverX woke in the bedroom of his penthouse on top of one of his many residential towers to what he thought was the sound of someone entering his room. It was only two days ago that Angel and Extonic had terrorized him and his people, and ever since then, SilverX became very paranoid. Reaching over to grab a dagger from his bed stand, SilverX intently searched the room for any sign of an intruder. As he touched the dagger, he knew he was already trapped. "What do you want?" he calmly asked as his heart tried to flee from its place in his chest.

"Very good," smirked a young man's voice. "You are as cunning as they say, but to answer your question, I just want to be paid."

SilverX could not see the man, but his voice came from the opposite side of the bed as his dagger he was reaching for. "Who sent you, and why?"

"You know better than to ask that." SilverX knew that he wouldn't answer the question, but he want to stall for time. "I was, however, given a message to tell you. It goes like this: like father, like son, a coup starts with a death." The assassin uncloaked to reveal that he was holding a sola gun to SilverX's head. "How would you like to do this?" he asked. "It's your choice."

As the man finished his sentence, another figure uncloaked next to him holding a sola gun to the assassin's head and another pointing at SilverX. "Not until he answers a few questions," commanded an indistinguishable electric voice.

The assassin raised his sola gun and empty hand in a surrendering motion and stated, "Go right ahead; I've got all night, and we don't need to worry about his guards; they're all dead."

"You actually missed a few," mocked the newer figure, "but they're taken care of." Redirecting, he continued, "SilverX, was that robot that was trying to kill Dariah yours?"

SilverX remained silent causing the figure to whack SilverX's shin with the sola gun, but as he did so, SilverX grabbed the dagger and drove it towards the figure's neck. Before he drove the killing blow into this figure, he noticed the assassin once again had his sola gun pressed to SilverX's head.

"We've reached a standstill," laughed SilverX.

"I wouldn't say that," stated the assassin, "since neither of us," he said nodding towards the mystery figure, "really wishes to kill the other. We just want information from you, and then I want to kill you."

"The information won't come if I'm going to die anyway. See, the only way this guy wins is if he kills you in order to guarantee that I won't die after forfeiting information to him," plotted SilverX. "Which is why he still has a sola gun to your head." The assassin started to feel uneasy. "You see, if you kill me, he'll kill you because he didn't get the information. If I kill him, you'll still kill me, and if he kills you, there is no one to stop me from killing him."

For the next six hours, the three of them were silent and still. As the sun started to creep through the window, the three persons looked over the other two without so much as moving their eyes or heads. Both the assassin and the mystery figure were wearing all black, but the assassin's face was visible.

"Cycro?" inquired the figure.

"Well, this is awkward," chuckled Cycro, somehow not upset his identity was known. "How do you know who I am?"

"Just trust me now; I'll explain everything after this is over. It is crucial that I get this information from SilverX before this world falls apart," explained the figure as he slowly redirected the sola gun pointed at Cycro towards SilverX who made no motion during the transition.

"Alright, you have twenty minutes, and if I don't get substantial evidence that this is important, I will kill him," bargained Cycro.

"Deal," agreed the figure. "SilverX," he started more firmly. "was that robot your doing?" SilverX lowered the dagger but did not respond. The figure put away the sola gun in his right hand and pulled out a dagger of his own which he ran up and down SilverX's leg. "Was it?" he enticed.

Hearing no response, the figure lifted the dagger and plunged it into SilverX's heel.

"Ahh," moaned SilverX, but he still did not answer the question so the figure rotated the dagger slowly.

Before the figure could repeat the question again, a burst of energy burned through the wall and struck the figure's head. The energy was absorbed by a shield that the figure wore, but the impact knocked him over falling behind Cycro. SilverX took the distraction as an opportunity to put his dagger into Cycro's stomach with such force, it caused him to trip over the figure that lay behind him. The figure, regaining composure, fired his sola gun back in the direction the one that hit him came from. SilverX rolled out of bed on the opposite side from Cycro and the other person and hurried to a cabinet in which held several of his own solas. As Cycro lay in pain, the figure scampered to his feet and fired a shot at the cabinet SilverX had opened destroying two sola guns but leaving a third intact. Having only one sola gun meant that SilverX had only one shot. Another shot burned through the wall but collided with no one. SilverX grabbed the one sola gun and dove to the ground by his bed where the figure could not see him. SilverX knew that this figure had used his two shots, but this man remained standing with both solas poised and ready to shoot. Then the man shot seven shots sweeping across the wall that the original attack came from. Ready to get away, the figure pulled out a grenade and threw it to the base of the window only five feet from SilverX. The figure darted to pick up Cycro as SilverX got to his feet and darted away from the grenade. The grenade went off as the figure, holding Cycro, sprinted towards the gaping hole. On the way, the figure grabbed the disgruntled SilverX, pulled him to his shoulder, and the three of them leaped out the thirtieth floor. On the way down, the figure cloaked the three of them and deployed a parachute to carry them safely to the ground.

On the ground, the figure handed Cycro SilverX's sola gun and said, "Watch him; I've got to get in contact with someone. I'd prefer to have him alive, but if he leaves you no choice go ahead and carry out your killing." Cycro couldn't move, but he held firmly to the sola gun pointed angrily at SilverX.

Chapter 21

"SilverX is losing focus," announced Edward, SilverX's top assistant, to a room crowded with thirty of SilverX's scientists, generals and close advisors. We completed the cyber, but he refuses to use it now. I believe he has lost sight of what Russia needs."

"He may not be fit to rule Russia any longer," included Dr. Land. "For a nation to be great, in this day and age, the rule of that state must be greater, and he must have no doubts that his actions are needed."

"Yeah!" erupted the audience.

"I was there," continued Dr. Land, "when SilverX overthrew his father Sil Marxiq, and once again it is time for Russia to name a new leader, and that leader is you Edward Sonisqua. With SilverX's death, Russia will follow you."

"I will not let Russia down," Edward assured.

"Now," started Dr. Land once again, "I give you the man who will aid us in this revolution, Cycro. Not only has he guaranteed the death of SilverX by eight in the morning tomorrow, but he has supplied us with five hundred sola guns and hundreds of heavy weapons such as tanks and rockets."

"Tomorrow," announced Cycro as he uncloaked next to Dr. Land, "Russia will be yours."

The room erupted in applause and cheers once more. Not one of those in the room doubted their actions. Each of them felt sure this coup was as simple as Dr. Land, Edward and Cycro had explained it to be.

"Generals, have your armies ready to go at eight A.M.," requested Edward, "and I want Cyber Beronith ready to fulfill my orders."

"Tomorrow will mark a new era for not only Russia, but planet Earth," assured Dr. Land. "Tomorrow!" he shouted over the increasingly loud cheers, "we declare our independence from Earth." The applause grew deafening as Dr. Land held his hand clenched in a fist high above his head.

Kyriac was awaken by a phone call from a frantic Karar. "Kyriac," she started, "I am in desperate need of help. I needed to get answers, so I broke into SilverX's house just as he was about to be assassinated. Now all of Russia is on lock down and it appears there is a coup d'état. I have SilverX and Cycro with me, but Cycro's hurt badly and SilverX can barely walk. We need to get out of here before we all die."

Kyriac knew there was no time for him to ask the hundreds of questions that emerged in his head, so he responded, "I'll see what I can do." After disengaging in the conversation with Karar, Kyriac immediately called Jev, explained the situation and pleaded for help.

"Kyriac, I can't help you," surrendered Jev. "The entire world is in chaos right now. Several cities were attacked and six council members have been assassinated. I am sorry, but I really cannot be of any assistance right now."

"Perhaps I can help," offered a voice behind Kyriac. Spinning around, he saw that it was Dariah. "After all, she is there partly because of me."

"Any help would be appreciated, Dariah. Thank you," thanked Kyriac, not questioning how or why Dariah was there at all.

"Don't thank me yet; this war has just begun. In my nightmares, we end up on opposite teams." Kyriac couldn't tell if Dariah was joking or not, and that scared him. "Come on," Dariah continued. "I have an aircraft outside." Kyriac grabbed his weapons and followed Dariah to his craft.

"SilverX," began Karar. "I need to know what's going on."

"It's a coup," struggled Cycro. Both Karar and SilverX looked over at Cycro. It's being led by Edward Sonisqua, and I'm the supplier."

"Edward?" gasped SilverX in disbelief. "My personal assistant?"

"They feel that, like your father, you have lost sight of what Russia needs.

I should also mention they are executing plan Apocalypse. They never fully explained it to me, but I understand that Russia is attempting to become the world leader instead of Earth by dissolving Earth's government."

"They would never have had the resources to execute that plan until they met you. How much weaponry did you give them?" demanded SilverX.

"They paid up front with some very nice technology. I don't know where they got it from, and I don't care. I know a good deal when I see it, but I honestly didn't think they had this much power," justified Cycro.

"Cycro, what did you give them?" insisted Karar.

"Five hundred solas from Amena along with a lot of heavy weaponry I've had stored up," answered Cycro.

"What could they have given you for that large amount of weapons?" requested Karar.

"Ten organic robots along with a new type of shield," replied Cycro.

"*Organic robots,*" thought SilverX. Realizing the danger, he gasped, "they have Cyber Beronith."

"What is that?" demanded Karar.

"It's an organic robot replication of the real Beronith using much of the real Beronith. He looks exactly the same, not like the cyber I made resembling Dariah. This one is much stronger. With the weapons you supplied, their shields, Cyber Beronith, and who knows how many more organic robots they may have created without my knowledge, I think they can easily take over Earth. We have to do something."

Kyriac and Dariah simultaneously bounded from the aircraft and down the desolate street, both wielding a sola gun in one hand and a sword glowing from the heat of their energy in the other.

"When did you learn that?" asked Kyriac, looking at the heated and glowing sword.

"Just a few days ago," responded Dariah as they rounded a corner straight into the sight of a group of soldiers. "Watch out!" he warned noticing the solas the soldiers were wielding. Both warriors ducked back around the corner before the group of soldiers could see who it was, hoping they didn't recognize Dariah's voice. "After seeing you do it, I kept trying until I figured it out," he continued explaining. He paused, and after several deep breaths, he continued. "We've got to fight them," he conceded. "Are you ready?"

Kyriac nodded, and they both turned around the corner and began firing. Each shot hit a soldier, but none of the soldiers fell. Seeing that their attack did not work, the two ducked into a building avoiding the tank fire that shredded the side of the building.

"They aren't using their solas," shouted Kyriac over the machine gun fire.

"They're one shot sola guns. If they fire and miss, they know they're dead for sure. They're going to wait until they can't miss.

As Dariah spoke, another group of soldiers rounded the same corner and fired upon the other group. The new group was much larger, but was getting mowed down without so much as hurting one of the original soldiers.

"While they're distracted, let's get past them," plotted Dariah.

The two burst out into the street at as fast of a sprint as they could, flying past the soldiers who originally fired at them. After only a few minutes of running, they arrived at Karar, Cycro and SilverX.

"We have to do something," warned SilverX as Kyriac and Dariah arrived.

"Come on, we have to get out of here," stated Dariah. "My aircraft was in low orbit while we got here. Let's find a safe place for it to land."

The five of them arrived at Jev's mansion and were greeted by thirty-five heavily armed soldiers who didn't like the fact that the people who had just arrived were more heavily armed than they were. With Jev's approval, the five of them were allowed in, weapons and all, excluding SilverX who came in with his arms bound.

They entered into a room in which Jev and several soldiers sat and watched numerous news stations on dozens of different screens.

"A coup was started by unknown members of SilverX's closest council... Several council leaders have been assassinated... The world waits in chaos as Guardian Jev has yet to act... Several European cities have been destroyed," Kyriac heard from the different stations as a shiver ran down his spine. "*The Unified Empire has helped nothing,*" he thought. "The world is in chaos," he heard again.

"Jev," started SilverX, but he was interrupted before he could continue.

"I don't want to hear it SilverX," blurted Jev. "A lot has happened in the last twelve hours, and I know much of it has to do with you. Even though you no longer lead them, I am sure much of what is happening was your idea."

"That is outrageous!" protested SilverX

"Is it?" inquired Karar now unmasked. "Last I knew, you seemed to know every detail about this operation except for the coup."

"Just because I knew about some of these plans doesn't mean that I organized them or planned to carry them out," argued SilverX. "I have done nothing wrong here; I am as much, if not more, a victim than any of you."

"Jev, it's time to address the world," informed a soldier that had just entered the room.

"Very well," said Jev who then proceeded over to a desk where Kyriac and Dariah were standing. The two of them started to move, but Jev motioned them to stay.

"Ladies and Gentlemen of Earth," Jev started, "I would like to say that I have good news; I would like to say this will be over momentarily, but that's just not the case. Russia has declared its independence, and members of the Russian military have overthrown the previous Russian leader Sil Marxiq or SilverX as most of you know him. They are now under the rule of a man named Edward Sonisqua, and under his control, they are attempting to overthrow the rest of Earth. Several councilmen have already died, so in order to preserve this nation, the remaining councilmen have relinquished all control temporarily to the Guardian, and subsequent succession, until this war is over. At which point, power will resume for the Council." He paused, and took an emotional breath. "A candle that burns wildly burns the fastest. This may be our gravest hour, but if we continue our hard work, peace will be restored. This Earth, our Earth, cannot tolerate those who cannot live peacefully with one another. Today, the grandest proponent of civil disobedience has reared its unfettering face on our burgeoning Empire. Tomorrow, that face will look up six feet and see the shovels of dirt as we bury his mutiny forever."

The world watched as Jev continued with his inspirational speech with Kyriac standing to his left and Dariah to his right. The two heroes of the world standing by Jev gave them hope beyond what just words could do.

"I urge all of you," he continued, "to stay calm during this." As the broadcast ended, Jev stood up and walked back over to where he was watching the news stations.

"Kyriac and I will go to Amena," suggested Karar. "They should be willing to help; after all, Kyriac is one of the highest ranked persons in their nation."

"For all we know, they could be supporting this attack," stated Jev.

"I can assure you that they are not," informed Cycro. "I provided all the weaponry for this assault. I will go with Karar and Kyriac back to Amena. I can pick up more weapons for you there."

"Fine, the three of you go," Jev commanded, "but if Cycro makes another mistake, make sure he can never make another." As he finished speaking, Kyriac, Karar, and Cycro exited the room. "Dariah and SilverX, can you two get rid of Edward?"

"I believe we can," responded SilverX. "I know Russia better than he does."

"I have new crafts for you two to use to get back in Russia. Since a helicopter would be easily targeted with a missile, these," Jev said pointing to a stack of three-inch-thick boards that looked like thicker, more rigid, surfboards. "Safin Boards will get you in and out less noticeably." The two of them walked over to the boards and tested them out. "They are very simple to use; you just lean. You can also lie on them to go faster than if you stand."

"I've got it figured out. Let's go," urged Dariah after only a few moments of experimenting on them.

"On second thought," stopped Jev. "SilverX, you stay here to help fight this operation Apocalypse since you know the plans. Dariah, you are on your own. SilverX and I will give you commands from here."

"No matter," assured Dariah. "I can capture him."

"You might need this," said Jev as he held out Dariah's sword. "I'm sorry that you have to fight again. If there was anyone else who could do this task…"

"It appears as though the peace I imagined is hopeless," interjected Dariah as he turned around and left with the Safin Board.

"Jev," began SilverX as soon as Dariah had left, "I don't think that you can win unless you use the Fuses. I mean…"

Jev cut him off. "The Fuses would only create more chaos, and we don't need more chaos now. We will not even discuss them again, understand?"

"So be it. In that case, you will need all you can get to strike in three locations: Multrop, Berlin and the coastal border between Russia and China. These locations will be struck next, if they haven't changed the plan. If they take these spots, they will control the seven points they need to wipe out the rest of Earth." After pausing, SilverX continued, "this isn't a takeover you know. They plan to wipe out everyone except Russia."

"Do they need all the points or do we need to stop them at one?" pressed Jev.

"With each point they hold, their ability to hold the Earth and the other points increases significantly. If you get every other point, they'll be no better than now; however, they need the area intact for their plan to work. If you were to entirely destroy these locations, their plan would fail. You'd then have them outnumbered and they'd be without their advantage."

"There are people in these places. I cannot just have them killed."

"They will die no matter what you do. Don't you understand Jev? They are not going to hesitate killing anyone."

"I will restrain from killing innocent people," assured Jev. "Find another way."

Having heard enough from Jev, SilverX said, "you're too soft to rule Earth," and he stormed out of the room.

"What is the plan?" requested a soldier as SilverX exited.

"We're going to Multrop. We can easily defend that and most of our forces are there already. Whatever troops we have outside of Multrop need to try to hold Berlin and Yainme, the city on the border of Russia and China." The soldier repeated the orders to his command. "prepare whatever aircraft we have to transport all of the troops, plans and equipment from this location to Multrop." The soldier repeated the orders once more, and within minutes, soldiers were hauling equipment out of the room. "Find SilverX and tell him we're going to Multrop."

"SilverX left sir, on a Safin Board."

"Where did he go?"

"I have no idea," admitted the soldier.

"*What are you going to do SilverX?*" pondered Jev.

Chapter 22

Kyriac had been twirling a dagger around his finger admiring the change in tone as the blade came towards him and receded away for fifteen minutes causing an annoyed Cycro to blurt, "would you stop that?" Kyriac abruptly stopped consequently causing the dagger to fall from his fingers to the floor by Cycro's foot where it stuck protruding inches from Cycro's foot.

Karar was piloting and thus paying no attention to those in the back. She, instead, was thinking more on what Amena could offer Earth since they had no army, and they vowed to stay out of Earth's wars. It had been decades since they even discussed military.

It wasn't five minutes later that the annoyed Cycro, worried Kyriac, and thoughtful Karar arrived at the port in Amena once again. This time, Karar didn't need to use the equipment to find the portal to Amena since she figured out the calculus that determined the portal's location. The three of them entered into a small doorway and emerged in the capital building as they had with Damien before.

"The council is probably in session right now. Kyriac, being a knight, you have access to the council," informed Karar.

The three of them stopped before a set of doors which Kyriac recognized from his first trip to Amena. Kyriac reached first for Karar's hand, and then with his other hand, he opened the door. As was the case with the last time he visited the council of Japan, Kyriac entered holding onto Karar's hand feeling comforted by her touch. Only this time, Kyriac wasn't afraid of those he saw on the other side of the door.

"Earth's problems are Earth's problems!" shouted one of the councilmen as the rest of the room quieted seeing Kyriac walk through the door. Damien turned to see Kyriac wearing the white armor that he had given him only weeks before. This time, he exuded confidence.

"I am pleased to see you once again Kyriac. We thought you had joined Earth permanently," laughed Damien. "However, I'm sure we all know why you are here, and we were discussing the war on Earth. Please, tell us what you know, and what you'd like for us to do, but I must warn you, we are limited in our ability to act."

Kyriac, with the help from Karar and Cycro, explained everything they knew about the war. "We request all the military support we can get," he concluded.

"I am sorry to have to tell you this Kyriac, but currently our military is fighting a much greater war supporting our friends, the Mascien Galaxy," Damien stated.

"*Military?"* thought Karar.

"Compared to this war," continued Damien, "the one on Earth seems insignificant. All we can do for you is provide refuge for those who wish to escape Earth as we have always done, unless you know of some other way we can help." The two of them argued for nearly a half an hour before things go so heated, Kyriac cried out, "how can you all abandon your own race? Billions of people could die!" Kyriac drew the energy to his hands causing the heat to swell to incredible temperatures. Karar pulled her hand away in pain as Kyriac's hands burst into flames. "Cowards like you don't deserve to hold my trust!" he cried.

"Cowards like you don't deserve to live!" cried Dariah as he fell from his board and plunged his sword into the chest of a soldier who was protecting the entrance to Edward Sonisqua's base.

Damien held out his hand towards Kyriac and he too burst his hands into flame, only Damien's fire spread over his entire body. "Kyriac," he said through the flame. "I am a pure Mascien. Stand down immediately or I will be forced to subdue you. You may be a strong human, but there is no human that can kill a Mascien. I have over ten times your strength. Now I say again, stand down."

It wasn't the words that Damien said that caused Kyriac to leave. It was the fact that he had assumed that Damien was human and a friend, and when he wasn't either, Kyriac felt betrayed and more disappointed than before. Karar and Cycro followed Kyriac out of the council chamber, and on the way out, the council remained silent, almost angry, as they too felt betrayed by the one they put so much hope in to.

After exhausting himself killing thirty soldiers, Dariah reached the front door to the base. Before he was able to attempt to break the door down, it opened to reveal a figure standing on the other side that Dariah recognized immediately.

"Beronith," Dariah whispered.

"Hello brother," laughed Beronith.

Upon arriving at his new base in Multrop, Jev saw on the broadcast screens SilverX ready to give his own speech. "This is a rogue broadcast," announced SilverX, "but I must give warning to the people of Earth. A deadly plan known as plan Apocalypse is being executed by those who once were part of my highest council. This plan calls for the chaotic extermination of all those who do not support their cause. I urge all of you to take up arms against these evil people. Your current Guardian cannot force himself to take the action necessary to stop this plan and Japan is refusing to send aid. We, the people of Earth, must stand together to stop this plan or we will all be exterminated."

"Stop this!" shouted Jev. "Someone stop this broadcast!"

"We don't know where he is!" admitted an officer.

"He's in outer space," cried another. "He's at a missile base currently above Europe!"

"Tell all the troops to move away from Berlin, he's going to bomb Berlin!" cried Jev.

"I take it upon myself to take every action needed to prevent the extermination of Earth. Casualties are to be expected, especially in this war. I kill a few to save many. When this war is over, remember the sacrifice Berlin made for us all." The broadcast ended, but each screen was brought to live footage of Berlin as missiles rained down onto the unsuspecting city completely destroying it and surrounding areas.

The world stood still for hours as missiles fell like raindrops on people who never had a chance to save themselves. They all watched in horror as millions of innocent people were killed without warning as part of SilverX's preventative measures against plan Apocalypse. After Berlin was reduced to ash, SilverX retook the screen. "These actions are necessary. Your Guardian Jev is protecting Multrop, but there is one more spot in which I need all of your help defending. Russia will attack Yainme tonight. I, as well as many of the Guardian's soldiers will be there, but I fear this will not be enough. Please, tonight, take part in the survival of this planet. Do not let them take Yainme! And, my beloved Russians, please stop this senseless violence. I know many of you have already stood up for me, but I ask all of you to stand up for Russia. This is not the Russia I know. We are above all this. I ask that you all cease this criminal act. I refuse to lose faith in you, and I know you are scared. We all are, but you're Russian, and we do not hesitate to do what is right." The broadcast screens went black. By this point, Jev was sitting in a chair with his left hand covering his eyes and his right hand supporting himself on his own knee.

"Sir, what should we do?" requested a soldier near Jev.

"Send any troops that escaped Berlin to Yainme, and all troops from this city to the wall. We'll hold this city; let us see if SilverX had any effect of Yainme's outcome. After Yainme, if anyone survives, bring SilverX into custody."

"Time to die brother!" shouted Beronith as he lunged for Dariah. In midair, Beronith drew two swords and swung them towards Dariah who blocked both with his one sword. The fire around his hands spread to his forearms and sword. Beronith pulled one sword away and swung it towards his brother. Dariah dodged backwards away from the oncoming attack.

"Kyriac, I need your help," cried Dariah into their communication system.

"I'm on my way," assured Kyriac now back from Amena. To Karar he said, "drop me off with Dariah. Then you two go help Jev. Go as fast as you can."

Karar nodded in agreement.

Beronith ran towards Dariah with one sword pointed straight outward. Dariah ran to his right and Beronith followed. When Beronith got closer, Dariah drew out a sola gun, swung around and fired at Beronith. The shot hit Beronith in the chest and knocked him onto his back, but he hit the ground with his swords and pushed himself back up. Beronith, once again, lunged for Dariah. Dariah put his sword up to block but right before Beronith reached Dariah, he stopped midair with a sword protruding from his back. Kyriac came uncloaked. Beronith looked at the sword going through him, looked at Kyriac, and looked at the sword again. After assessing the situation, Beronith kicked Kyriac in the face sending him backward into Dariah. Beronith landed on his other foot and removed the sword from his stomach. Back on his feet, Dariah swung his sword for Beronith's head, but Beronith blocked using Kyriac's sword. Dariah grew angrier and the flame extended past his shoulders and met in the middle of his back and chest. The fire then covered his entire body. Beronith couldn't hold back Dariah's attack any longer, and the sword he held was forced against his own chest and neck. Dariah quickly drew his sword back and thrust it forward impaling Beronith's throat. By this point, Kyriac was also standing again.

"Was that...?" started Kyriac.

"Yeah," responded Dariah. "SilverX brought him back to life using robot parts, but he was only partially my brother. I had no choice brother. I saw you die, and now I kill you myself."

"Are you alright?" inquired Kyriac.

"I am fine," assured Dariah as he handed Kyriac his sword. "I have to finish up here, but SilverX will need your help at Yainme. Take my Safin Board and help him."

Kyriac nodded in agreement and left.

"What is that?" demanded one of the soldiers in Jev's command post pointing to a section of America that suddenly lost all sensors.

"Get me satellite visual of that area," commanded Jev and his soldiers obeyed. On one of the screens, the image of thousands of tiny marble-sized robots swarmed about. "It's the Fuses, but how?" As if on cue, Karar and Cycro entered into the command to view the Fuses along with Jev.

"It's got to be that doctor," predicted Cycro.

"What doctor?" Karar and Jev asked simultaneously.

"His name was Dr. Land," Cycro replied.

Karar and Jev looked at each other, and both then looked to the screen. "We have less than a half-hour to get as many people as we can to Amena. Get as many soldiers to help evacuate as we can spare," Jev ordered.

Dariah ran through the complex killing anyone he saw until he finally reached the entrance to the main control center. The fire still engulfed Dariah as he barged through the door.

"SilverX," started Kyriac, now close enough to SilverX to be able to draw his attention. "I've come to help you."

"You've come just in time," assured SilverX, but he was cut off as sola gun and tank fire started bombarding their location. Kyriac focused his energy about his body creating whirls of fire swirling around him. He then pulled one hand in front of his face to admire the flame. While admiring the flame, a sola gun shell exploded on his hand sending Kyriac falling backwards. The blast also caused Kyriac's electronic shield on his wrist to explode unable to take the full force of the blast. Due to the fact that the blast was so close to his face, Kyriac absorbed the remainder of the energy in his face and head. Dizzy, Kyriac stumbled back to his feet, brushed himself off and tried to open his eyes to find they were already open. Kyriac was blind. A shiver ran down his spine as the thought *"oh god, what's happened?"* "My eyes!" he cried aloud and reached for his now broken eyes. He tried to cry but could not. He clawed at them, hoping they were covered. There were only bloody recesses left where his eyes were.

"Kyriac?" questioned SilverX nervously.

"I'm blind," Kyriac cried. "I'm blind, I'm blind, I'm blind..." Kyriac trailed off as he lost his ability to speak choked by a massive lump in his throat. Kyriac fell to his knees slowly losing his ability to breathe.

Realizing the severity of the situation, two people rushed to help Kyriac up.

"Leave him," ordered SilverX with a sola gun pointed towards one of those who rushed over. An explosion occurred ten feet from SilverX sending debris towards him, but he didn't flinch as the stones struck him. "Kyriac, you can still fight. Your eyes were only one of your senses. You're a fighter, now prove to us how strong you really are and stand up. Focus on your other senses instead of your eyes. Focus on hearing and touch for they will get you through this." The words entered Kyriac's ears and touched his soul. He stood up and looked towards SilverX without the ability to see him. He pushed his shoulders back and breathed in deeply. "Now," continued SilverX. "can you determine where I am?" Kyriac nodded. "Show me," SilverX insisted, and Kyriac drew his sword and placed the blade at SilverX's throat. "Good," SilverX whispered as Kyriac withdrew his sword. "I know what you're capable of better than most. Concentrate real hard, and you will be able to see, but with your ears."

Kyriac once again drew his energy from within him creating fire flowing about him, but this time the fire burned hotter, glowing a yellowish green color instead of the red it glowed before. Another sola gunshot flew by Kyriac just grazing him on the way, but the energy didn't damage him.

"*The energy around him protects him*", thought SilverX. "*He is invincible. Not even the sola guns can hurt him.*"

As he entered the room, Dariah was bombarded by sola gun fire causing his electronic armor shield to overload, as Kyriac's had, from the surplus of energy and explode. As it did so, Dariah too erupted into green flame. Everything around him started melting or burning from his heat. After the sola gun fire stopped, a green glow could be seen through the smoky and burning room. With no ammunition or hope of escape, the soldiers protecting Edward Sonisqua, placed their weapons on the ground and held their hands in the air. Dariah ignored their plea.

"You think because you lay down your weapons after you fail to kill me that you should be spared. Spared for what?" he demanded as he ran his sword through the first defenseless soldier. "So you can kill again." He stabbed another. "You're a plague." Another. "You take life, but when it's your turn to die, you cower." Another. "Fighting comes with a heavy burden." Another. "And, I'll make everyone pay it."

“The Fuses are here!” announced a soldier.

“Get everyone out of here! Come with me Karar and Cycro; we must leave,” Jev urged, and as he finished a deafening low pitch noise overtook the city, shaking the room they were in.

“You go,” suggested Cycro, “I’ll stay here. Let this be my repayment.”

“What?” asked Karar.

“I stole twelve Mascien fleet carriers to aid us here.” Karar opened her mouth to speak, but Cycro stopped her. “Get out of here while you can!”

“Thank you,” mouthed Karar as she and Jev left.

“I’ll buy you as much time as I can before hell breaks loose here,” assured Cycro on their way out.

“SilverX, how are things at Yainme?” Jev asked into an intercom.

As Kyriac’s sword cut through another soldier, SilverX responded, “Kyriac has lost his sight, but he is still alive and fighting stronger than ever. I believe with him here, we will win.”

“Kyriac,” whispered Karar while exhaling all the air from her lungs with no desire to breathe the air back in. Coldness was brought over her body.

“We’re on our way to get you and Kyriac off this planet,” informed Jev. “The Fuses have been activated and they’re at Multrop right now.”

“That’s not part of the plan,” SilverX argued.

“I know,” Jev responded. “I know…”

Every soldier and civilian on the base lay dead except the one he left to tell the story, but Dariah’s thirst to kill was not quelled. He returned to the surface to search for other victims. “Anyone who fights is an enemy,” he assured himself. As he said this, he heard Jev and SilverX speaking, and he knew where he would go.

The armies at Yainme were retreating from the force that SilverX and Kyriac had aided just as Jev and the now sobbing Karar arrived.

"Kyriac!" cried Karar as she dashed out of the helicopter and threw her arms around Kyriac. "Oh Kyriac," she sobbed as she put her face into his chest.

"Come," shouted Jev, "we have to leave now." Kyriac and Karar entered the helicopter, but SilverX remained.

"This is my mess," he said. "I'm going to stick around to help clean it up."

Jev didn't argue as he lifted into the air without SilverX. SilverX watched them until they were out of sight, and when they were, a new figure entered the battlefield.

"SilverX," Dariah shouted. "You've ruined my life and the lives of millions. For that you pay with your life."

"I will not, Dariah," he said with no hesitation. "I am and always will be your master."

"I have no master," Dariah cried as he lunged for SilverX, creating the green flames around him that he had before. SilverX slashed his Safin Spear at Dariah, but it melted away when it reached the flames. His eyes widened as he felt Dariah's sword enter his chest. Before SilverX was able to pass into death, Dariah whispered, "you will be my slave in the afterlife," and he turned his sword and thrust it out from SilverX's chest letting him dropped to the ground. On the way down, Dariah spun around and decapitated the already deceased SilverX. "Are you listening Kyriac?" he spoke into his intercom. "I will meet you at Multrop. We can settle this war now."

"I will go to Multrop," Kyriac firmly stated.

"Kyriac, Dariah's crazy," Jev warned him.

"I know that," Kyriac responded.

"No please," Karar whispered.

"I will go."

"If you could see, you would see my tears," whispered Karar. "You would see how much this hurts me." Karar stared at the floor without so much as motioning towards Kyriac. More tears formed in her eyes.

"It's something I have to do. I have to," said Kyriac in a gentle voice and then added, "they need me."

"I need you. I need you here with me. No more fighting," Karar cried.

"Don't fight anymore. This world has only caused you pain. Why do you need to rescue them when you owe them nothing? How can you be so selfless?"

"I need to."

Instead of responding, Karar ran over to Kyriac and grabbed his hand. "Don't go," she sobbed.

"I must," replied Kyriac.

Karar held his hand tighter saying, "but you'll die if you go," and she turned his hand palm towards the heavens as a tear fell from her face and landed in his hand. "I can't live without you. Please, please, I beg you."

Kyriac pulled Karar close and gently said, "I have to go; it is not something I want to do, but the people of Earth need me. I can't let millions of people die. I must go now."

"No...," whispered Karar into Kyriac's chest as the tears began flowing from her eyes leaving a puddle of tears on Kyriac's shoulder.

Kyriac pulled away, but Karar held him tighter. Kyriac gently pushed Karar back and turned around. He walked to the door of the now landed helicopter, looked back with only tears of blood in his bloody eyes, and started towards the battle against a person that, only hours ago, he wanted to call his friend.

Jev had landed close enough to Multrop that Kyriac was able to run to where Dariah was waiting for him.

"You've finally arrived, Kyriac. I was wondering how long you would take, or if you were going to show up at all," shouted Dariah.

The Fuses swarmed around Dariah while the Mascien carriers hovered above Kyriac, both poised to attack the other. As the two stood determining how they would attack, a familiar hand placed itself in Kyriac's.

"No," whispered Kyriac, "you should not be here. It is dangerous."

"I couldn't let you do this alone," Karar choked out with a tear running down her cheek and a lump in her throat, knowing that they were both about to die.

"Either you help me, or you die," instructed Dariah. "You know fighting leads to more fighting, yet that's all you seem to be able to do. I have dreams Kyriac, and in those dreams, I see you're the answer. Everyone looks to you, and you fight. Your existence makes them want to fight more. Help me Kyriac. I swear to you, this is the only way to save this universe.

We have to show people that if they fight, they will die. Punish those who fight with me, or be punished yourself."

"That's not the only way," argued Kyriac. "It can't be."

"But it is. Will you join me or not?" begged Dariah.

"You know I can't. I can't do what you're asking," wailed Kyriac. "I can only show you that you're wrong."

Letting go of Karar's hand, Kyriac bolted forward and erupted into a brilliant blue flame. Karar started crying more heavily as Kyriac pulled out his daggers and sword, and Dariah simultaneously drew his sword. Kyriac reached Dariah and was met by Dariah's sword in his stomach. Instead of defending, Kyriac lodged one of his daggers into Dariah's neck. The area erupted in explosions as the carriers engaged the Fuses. Dariah stumbled backwards with a dagger in his neck. Quickly, he removed it from his neck allowing his body to start to heal the wound. He looked towards Kyriac who knelt using Dariah's sword, embedded in him, as support to hold him slightly upright. Dariah laughed as he pulled a sola gun from his belt. Reaching Kyriac, he was greeted by Kyriac's other dagger, but he grabbed the attacking hand preventing Kyriac from placing another dagger in his neck. Dariah pulled the weakened Kyriac up by that arm, removed the sword from his stomach, placed the sola gun in the wound facing upward, and fired killing Kyriac with a blast upward through his chest, neck and head.

Before he hit the ground, Karar felt his death. Her knees and lungs failed to work. She choked and cried until Dariah approached. She tried to be strong but was unable. Dariah stood above her and plummeted Kyriac's sword mercilessly into the sobbing Karar, hunched over in a pool of her own blood and tears.

"Death is better than suffering," he coldly stated as he walked away leaving her hunched over with a sword protruding from her dead body with her tears creating ripples in the puddle of blood that formed beneath her body.

Chapter 23

Jev spent as long as he could helping people from Earth hoping Kyriac or Karar would arrive, but they never came. He knew the worst had happened.

Several million people had escaped Earth and arrived in Amena before Damien decided it was too dangerous for them to keep the portals open. Among those who made it through was Cycro; however, he made it through carried by one of his colleagues, Eric. When they arrived, they were both arrested.

Days passed and Jev was working with a few scientists and politicians determining where the people of Earth could relocate and how much it would cost when Damien arrived.

Approaching Jev, Damien requested, "may I speak with you Jev," and he motioned towards the hallway from which he came. Jev nodded and followed Damien into the hall. "Jev, I've prepared locations where your people may stay on a more permanent basis. I understand that settling a new area or planet may take years, so I've tried to do my part in making your stay comfortable."

"It should only take weeks with the technology and capital that we've got here," informed Jev.

"Something more pressing has come up, so your relocation must be put aside for a while. You understand, don't you?"

"No, I don't understand. What could be more pressing than the lives of over forty million people?" Jev pressed firmly.

"The lives of billions, actually," he answered. "Let me tell you something which I sincerely hope you decide to keep to yourself. With Earth no longer holding ties to Amena, the Mascien Galaxy has declared Amena its own State, so we must elect the first Supreme Guardian. Do you understand now?"

"You want my people to vote for you?" Jev asked, and Damien nodded. "What if all my people vote for me?"

"They cannot," Damien informed, "because you are neither human, nor Mascien; however as Supreme Guardian, I would be able to appoint you Guardian of a colony founded by Amena, if you know what I mean."

"What if I expose you? You can't win then."

"All that capital and technology you were talking about all belongs to me. If I don't become Supreme Guardian, you will not get a new home." Jev clenched his fists as Damien began to walk away, but Damien stopped, turned around and then added, "there is someone we have locked up that has been demanding to see you. I suppose you should visit him before he is put to death. You know Cycro, right? I'll lead you there if you wish to see him." Damien looked at Jev to see him staring back angrily. "Follow me," he added.

A few minutes later, Jev and Damien arrived in a hallway with small enclosures on either side in which people resided locked away, awaiting execution. "There is no reason that you should hate me Jev; after all, I am still helping you and your people," Damien said while walking. "Is it so much to ask for something in return? While we wait for the election, I will give all of your people jobs primarily working on construction, construction for your planet, in which, I will pay them enough to live off of." Every word Damien said made Jev hate him more.

They arrived at Cycro's cell who waited to see who was walking by in an attempt to save himself from the immense boredom that had taken him. Jev looked upon the hopeless and beaten Cycro with angry eyes, not anger for Cycro anymore, but from his now unrighteous and self-oriented friend, Damien.

"Jev," mustered Cycro now filled with hope. "It is good to see you."

"I have things to do," stated Damien. "I will leave you two."

"What happened?" demanded Jev after Damien had left. "What happened to Kyriac, Dariah, and Karar or Earth?"

With a noticeably different and more cheerful tone, Cycro responded,

"I don't know the fate of Earth, but I can tell you the rest. Kyriac is dead by Dariah's hand. Dariah, the Russian army and the Fuses were all still around when I left. Karar, however, is alive and safe. She was almost dead when I took her. Dariah stabbed Kyriac's sword into her and left it there, so I've come into possession of that too. Karar is now with as many people as I could save before we left Earth. I managed to keep four of the Mascien Battle Cruisers, and that is where these people are currently living while we build homes on a new planet. I won't tell you where it is because I don't want the Masciens to know, but I will come back when it is safe to tell you. Now, I should be going." As he said the last sentence, Cycro's cell opened to allow him to leave and a figure carrying two solas, cloaking devices, electronic shields and Safin Boards walked up to them. The figure unsheathed a sword and held it out for Jev to take. Jev recognized it immediately as Kyriac's sword. "Telling you these things and giving you his sword were the only reasons that I came to Amena. I'll see you later," he said before he disappeared.

Jev simply smiled seeing the ease in which Cycro escaped from a Mascien holding cell also knowing that he would suffer no consequence for fear of jeopardizing Damien's chance of becoming Supreme Guardian.

Chapter 24

"Talum and Roqu have been destroyed," informed Mascien Lieutenant Tali to his commander So'Sol. "That leaves this as the only city we have left on this planet."

"Screw the Mascien Defensive Force!" cursed So'Sol as he pounded his fist against his table. "They told us to hold this planet despite the odds and they give us no aid, nor a way to evacuate."

"It appears as though we will all die here," informed Tali.

"If it comes near that, I have a private ship. We might be able to make it past their battleships in orbit, but let us hope it does not come to that."

"Yes, let us hope."

Meanwhile, in the soldiers living area, several soldiers gathered around a heater to talk about the new human soldiers that had joined their army that day.

"What good will humans do here? They're so weak, they'll just get in the way," proclaimed one soldier.

"They're completely worthless," exclaimed another.

"We're not as worthless as you make us to be," interrupted a human. "My name is Dija. I am captain of the human squad here known as Kyriac's Knights. We're not here to be thrown aside. We are an elite group here to uphold something that Kyriac started, and that is his selfless protection of all mankind. He died ensuring that we survive, and each one of us is willing to do the same. I ask that you not underestimate us, and we will not disappoint you."

"Wow," commented the first Mascien soldier, "did you practice that speech all day?" The other soldiers laughed.

"We've come with our own weapons, armor and provisions; the least you could do is respect us for coming to help you," replied Dija. "Dariah is all of our enemy."

"We don't need help from humans," boasted the soldier with an emphasis on the word 'humans.' By this point, a large crowd of Mascien and human soldiers had gathered to see what the commotion was about. "Allow me to introduce myself: I am Ardion, captain of the White Crystal Lords."

"Go back to Earth, humans!" shouted a member of the crowd.

"It is obvious that you're not wanted here; why don't you pack up and go home?" suggested Ardion.

"Because, we humans no longer have a home," Dija replied as he turned around and led the humans back to their camp. One human remained a few seconds longer than the rest. He stared straight into the eyes of Ardion, as wild animals do to challenge one another. This particular human wore a black layer of clothing over his face and body. His eyes shown through, revealing a brilliant shade of blue, the shade of which was rarely found in people who have lived through any hardship. The clothes he wore covered an obviously well-built body that made any other person on this planet appear feeble. Ardion laughed at him, but even this Mascien couldn't hide the fear this person put in him as his laugh came from not his belly, but from the back of his throat where his vocal cords became choked and knotted. "*Who is that?*" he thought before asking it aloud.

The answer came from an unexpected source, "his name is Xoz," So'Sol responded. "And you better watch out for him; he holds the highest recorded human score on the physical fitness test, a 792. As I recall, Ardion, you had an 816. I haven't ever seen a human score above one hundred, but each and every one of these humans scored higher than two hundred, with Xoz holding the highest. It would appear that these humans aren't so weak anymore."

"What are our orders, sir? Are we going to send aid to Roqu or Talum?" asked Ardion, now standing at attention.

"No," replied So'Sol. "Both Roqu and Talum have been destroyed. "Our orders are to defend this planet while we build an offensive to retake Roqu."

"How is that possible?" demanded Ardion.

"I don't know, but these are our orders. Now get your men ready. The enemy force is bound to arrive within a couple of hours. I am putting the White Crystal Lords up on the front wall and the Kyriac Knights in the gate. You two need to coordinate the protection of the entrance."

"But, sir, they're human," argued Ardion.

"I am quite aware of that, but I need them there. The White Crystal Lords are the best troop I have, so that's why I'm pairing you up with the humans. If we lose the gate, it will be your fault, understand?"

"Of course sir," Ardion replied.

"Not that it'll matter whose fault," So'Sol muttered as he walked away.

"It's been over a year now," argued Jev. "We've got our planet and moon completely built far beyond how many people we have. You've been elected as Supreme Guardian, so it would appear as though my half of the bargain is complete."

"Patience Jev," responded Damien. "Please have patience and wait for the correct time."

"What correct time?" pressed Jev. "We're ready to leave now."

"Jev, we do not have enough ships to bring your people to Threna."

"What do you mean? We had a deal." Jev's voice was getting heated.

"Since you are now part of my political council, I'll let you in on something: we're losing the war we started"

"Of course you are," replied Jev. "You openly attack anyone who isn't Mascien or human. That makes over a dozen other races that you're warring with."

"I don't need your advice, Jev. They know nothing of this planet or of Threna, so we've built a massive counter-attack that we just sent a week ago. Even though a few of our planets are still bound to fall, this attack will turn the war. I ask that you wait until after this war to settle your new planet," urged Damien.

"No," Jev stated. "With people like you commanding this war, it will be a war that lasts an eternity. My people will not wait that long."

"It would appear as though there is a lack of ships here," started a new person who had just entered the room. "Perhaps I can help." The figure removed his hood to reveal that it was Cycro, smiling cockily at Damien.

"You see, with the help of some of Damien's enemies, the Guild has become very powerful. Neither of you know where that is, but I think that for now, it's better that way; however, I can transport all of your people in one trip along with provisions that Damien will be supplying?" Cycro looked towards Damien to finish his question not at all certain if Damien was supplying provisions. "I took the liberty of arriving at this planet after the entire military left, just in case I'm still wanted."

"You are still wanted, and I will arrest you," informed Damien.

"I don't think so," Cycro boasted as he lifted his right hand, revealing he was carrying a new type of sola gun. "See this sola gun? Not even Kyriac's energy would protect him."

"It still only takes me one shot to take care of you," Damien stated while he raised his own sola gun and aimed it at Cycro.

Cycro chuckled before he started speaking. "What you mean is you still only have one shot, and please enlighten me: shoot me." Without thinking Damien obeyed, and the full blast from the sola gun was absorbed by Cycro's electronic shield without damaging him. "Now that you are no longer armed, Jev, my ships are waiting. We're ready to take you aboard."

"Thank you, Cycro."

"I believe that I probably owe you one or two, so let's call us even, and Damien, if you wanted to load some provisions, you can do that too," laughed Cycro. "I brought some in the probable chance that you won't respect any part of your promise, and by 'brought them,' I mean we've been raiding your planet for several hours now. You really have no effective police force here."

"You trashy thief, Cycro," cursed Damien.

"Mascien," Cycro retorted. "A cowardly one on top of that."

Two hours passed before they could see the opposing army. As the army approached, those commanding the gate opened it allowing one human to go through. "What are they doing?" asked Ardion to So'Sol.

"Killing one of their own it would appear," responded So'Sol before he realized that it was Xoz that they had let through. By this point, the gate was closed, and Xoz was fifty feet away from the gate and sixty feet closer to the oncoming army. He unsheathed his two swords and took off running together towards the army.

"Ready your solas!" shouted Dija. "Aim away from Xoz, he'll take care of himself."

Within a second of Xoz colliding with the enemy wall, ten enemy soldiers were dead, but it took three before any one of them hit the ground.

"Fire!" commanded Dija as the one hundred and fifty Kyriac Knights fired upon every enemy they could, except those near Xoz leaving the Mascien ground troops unable to do anything while the enemy was out of range of everything but the single shot sola guns they had. The only effective weapon the Masciens had at this point was the massive sola gun cannons, but most of them were occupied combating the air assault.

"The enemy is beginning their retreat!" announced So'Sol, after only twenty minutes of fighting.

With a signal from Dija, four of the Kyriac's Knights got on Safin Boards and took off to the retreating soldiers picking off as many enemies as they could. In a panic, the enemy ran in all directions. Responding, the remaining Kyriac's Knights got on boards to surround the enemy. Slowly, they worked their way inward to where Xoz was still battling without a shield or armor as though he wanted to die. When the last enemy had fallen, he looked up to see Dija holding a board for him. Beyond Dija, he saw an enemy ship descending towards them. Dija saw the trouble in his eyes and looked up to see the ship as well. "All Kyriac's Knights back!" he shouted, but his voice was drown out by a deafening crack as several missiles ripped through the atmosphere towards the ship. The missiles didn't come from the planet, rather the other side of the planet. As the Kyriac's Knights retreated, pieces of the enemy ship plummeted to the ground as forty Mascien battleships came into view firing relentlessly upon the enemy ship. Within seconds, the enemy ship was torn to pieces without so much as damaging the Mascien fleet.

"I'm glad we made it in time," came a voice from one of the ships. "I am Yemzi, commander of this fleet sent by Amena under the command of Supreme Guardian Damien. This planet will be liberated shortly."

"Looks like we're no longer needed here," Dija pointed out to his soldiers. "Let's pack up and head back home to get new orders."

Chapter 25

"Cycro," began Dija. "I've come to report that the Kyriac's Knights have completed our mission, and we are ready for our next task."

"Make sure that Jev and his people are settled in and recruit more members from them if you can. After that, travel to the Arachor world of Deltu. I learned from a few Mascien soldiers that when they arrived at Deltu, with the intent to conquer it, it had been completely destroyed. They said it was the work of Dariah. Report anything you find on that planet to me immediately."

"We will not betray the ideals of Kyriac, the Kyriac's Knights will not let you down." Dija bowed and exited the room leaving Cycro alone to think.

"I am sorry Kyriac. It wasn't Dariah that killed you. It was because of me. I caused all this mess."

"Am I interrupting anything?" Jev asked as he entered the room.

"No," responded Cycro in a quiet, saddened, voice. "I was just thinking."

"Dija spoke with me on his way out. Thank you once again, Cycro."

"Please don't thank me. All of this is my fault."

"What happened to Kyriac was not your fault, and you've done more than enough to preserve his memory. I will not hold you responsible for what happened on Earth. Dr. Land was going to do what he did regardless of what role you played. Because of you, we knew what was coming and were able to save millions. Your people obviously accepted that you've done right."

"Still, I feel responsible for it all," Cycro spoke very softly," Kyriac brings us hope even in death. He was, by far, the most selfless person I have ever met. Why did we get him killed Jev?"

"I guess we truly believed he could mend all of our problems for us; instead, he showed us that we must mend each other's."

"God, I wish he were here, so that I may apologize, and seek his forgiveness. When our gods abandoned us, all we had was Kyriac. We all looked to him as though he was a god, but in truth, he was still a boy."

"How is Karar?" Jev inquired in an attempt to change the subject.

"She blames me for all of this," Cycro responded. "Did you know they were in love?"

"I had a feeling."

"Well, now Karar will not speak to me or even come near me. She and a large group of people have left here and settled on another planet.

"With the boundaries of Earth no longer holding us together, we are bound to spread ourselves thin across the galaxy," Jev predicted. "We now live on Amena, some probably still on Earth somewhere, Threna, here on Terra, and Karar's planet."

"Armonia," Cycro included.

"You both chose Latin for your planet names," Jev pointed out.

"Yes, Earth and Harmony," Cycro added. "What does your planet stand for?"

"It's some ancient Mascien word that means second chances, so I am told."

"Why don't you rename it?"

"Because we're a colony under control of Supreme Guardian Damien," Jev informed with an attempted sarcastic tone place on 'Supreme Guardian.' "I should probably head back before they notice I am missing."

"Before you go, Jev," started Cycro. "I am going to Earth when Dija and his men get back. While I'm there, I'll search for people, but the main reason that I'm going is to build two monuments for Kyriac. One where he died and the other on that island where he trained."

"That sounds nice," Jev said while turning to leave.

"I want to place his sword there. Do you carry it still?" Cycro nodded at the sheathed sword on Jev's belt.

"Yes," said Jev as he handed the sword to Cycro.

"Oh and Jev," Cycro stated stopping Jev from leaving once again," stop in more often from now on. It's nice to be able to talk with you."

"With the portal network that you've set up, It'll be easier now. Cycro, these events cannot be blamed on any one person's actions, but rather the collective actions of all persons over the course of the last two-hundred years. Remember this," and Jev left leaving Cycro to play with these words in his mind.

Chapter 26

"Cycro, I don't think this was Dariah that destroyed Deltu," reported Dija now on the surface of Deltu with the Kyriac Knights. Xoz was absent on this mission because he needed to take a break after the last one.

"Are you sure?" Cycro inquired.

"From prior reports, I've recognized the damage and destruction that Dariah had left behind," Dija explained. "He always left an image for others to view to enforce his power; however, there is absolutely nothing left on this planet. We've run tests, and there are no residual chemicals, nanobots or radiation. All that is here is dirt. There's nothing; no energy; no life; no plants; absolutely nothing."

"Alright," acknowledged Cycro. "I'll contact you again in a couple of hours. For now, pack up and head back here."

"Yes sir," responded Dija.

"Which one of you is Xoz?" demanded a man among the Kyriac Knights who was not a part of their group.

"Who are you?" demanded Dija.

"After all I've done for Earth, you don't recognize me," moped the man. "I'm Dr. Land."

"You," scowled Dija. "What do you want here?"

"I want to see Xoz for myself," explained Dr. Land. "He reminds me of someone that I watched die. He fights with the same sort of passion as Kyriac did. You all still remember Kyriac, right? It is my belief that this Xoz is actually stronger than Kyriac was, but I wanted to meet him to be sure."

"You destroyed Earth and murdered Kyriac," accused Dija. "It is our duty to ensure that a man like you is not allowed to live on."

"I did not," mocked Dr. Land. "Dariah did both those things. I merely provided a catalyst to further the advancement of the human race. Look at how advanced we are now thanks to me."

"You've caused the destruction of the human race, not the advancement," Dija yelled.

"It is only in catastrophe that the human race is able to thrive to its true potential. Without this, Damien would've conquered Earth. Now, you have the means to defend against any Mascien attack. You should be thanking me, not accusing me."

"You killed billions, and for that, you need to be punished. Kill him," commanded Dija. Torscula pulled a sola gun from his belt and placed it pointed at Dr. Land's head.

"By killing me, you will only cause the destruction of yourselves. The Fuses can only be stopped by me.

"You're wrong," stated Torscula as he pulled the trigger. A bright light radiated from where the sola gun shot hit Dr. Land blinding all the members of the Kyriac's Knights temporarily. When their vision returned, Dr. Land was hovering fifty feet in the air with thousands of Fuses rapidly circling him creating an artificial gravitational center holding Dr. Land in the air.

As Dr. Land laughed hysterically, "Did I mention your little toys cannot kill me?" the Kyriac's Knights started hearing their most feared noise, the weak buzz of a Fuse, but millions of them together creating an irritating reverberation.

"I won't stand for the day a little machine can kill a human being," cried Marth, a young boy about the same age as Kyriac was when he was first discovered by Ice years ago. This warrior had been with the Kyriac's Knights since their start, but this was the first time he had spoken up. "I just won't," he repeated as the Fuses slowly approached. His head never looked up as he spoke. He stared, deep in thought, at the ground just in front of his feet, goose bumps running up his arms visible to those near him. When the Fuses were within fifty feet of the warriors, all prepared to battle, Marth cried out lifting his head high into the air and flinging his arms outward, "No!" As though a wall hit the fuses, they were forced backwards completely crushing the front ones, but the fuse army continued forward towards the warriors.

"Not today!" Marth cried out straining his body once again to push the fuses back. "Not ever!" he shouted firing his body again. In between each flare, Marth breathed heavily and hunched over trying to regain his strength. It was obvious that each time Marth did this attack, he used nearly everything that he had in his body. The Kyriac's Knights watched as wave after wave of fuses was pushed back by this unrelenting child, and wave after wave, Marth grew weaker.

The Kyriac's Knights were torn between sympathy, fear and hope in a blend of emotion unfelt by this elite team of the human race's best fighters. Many started to feel the pain from Marth just by watching, knowing the amount of pain and exhaustion he must be feeling.

Dija stood awestricken. In his many years and everything he had seen, he had never seen what Marth was doing. Somehow, Marth was sending a sphere of energy out from his body without hitting any of the other warriors, and the amount of energy needed to be able to do the kind of damage he was doing was insurmountable, far more than any other human, including Kyriac.

Like water crashing against a steel barrier, the fuses were destroyed without any progress towards the warriors until there weren't enough of them left to stage an attack against the Kyriac's Knights. Dr. Land, furious and scared for his own life, surrounded himself with the remaining Fuse army as he retreated as fast as he could into nearby mountains. The Kyriac's Knights didn't follow. Every one of them quickly attended to Marth, collapsed on the ground.

"Marth," whispered Dija into Marth's ear so quiet no one else could hear. "If you can hear me, open your soul. I can revive you. I owe you my life, and that's what I'm about to give you. You sacrificed yourself to save us all, but that's not a sacrifice you should have to make. This war isn't your doing, it's mine. Please open your soul; let me in. I can save you still."

Marth opened his eyes briefly, long enough to look Dija straight in the eyes. "I can't ask you for your life," he said.

By this point, their ship had landed on the planet to pick the warriors back up. "Quickly, let's get him onto the ship and attended to. Don't let him die. He shouldn't have to die. Don't let him."

"Cycro," Dija started up over his communication device. "We were attacked by the Fuse army commanded by Dr. Land. He is still on this planet. Get your military here to catch him. He's not getting off this planet, and his fuse army is not strong enough to do anything right now."

"It's on the way," Cycro responded.

"One more thing," Dija included, "one of our men is in critical condition. He did something I've never seen before and I don't know what it's done to his body, but he destroyed nearly the entire fuse army, and it was as big as we've seen it. Somehow, the fuses weren't able to get near us because of Marth. I guess what I'm trying to say is we need whatever medical and scientific resources you have to save this kid."

"I'll send what I've got, and I'll try to get Karar to help."

"Thank you Cycro," Dija thanked.

Chapter 27

The CelDes race was renowned for their amazingly ruthless biological concoctions that they'd release on enemy planets. Because of this, the Masciens developed tiny devices that would combat anything harmful introduced into a planet's ecosystem. These were implemented at all Mascien planets, spaceports and any military station; however, the Masciens didn't share this particular technology with any human planets, such as the one the CelDes were currently heading towards.

"Listen to me," pleaded Jev communicating with the commander of the CelDes fleet. "We're not allied with the Masciens. We're not at war with you. There are millions of people here that do not need to die."

"We've captured Amena, so we know your ties to them," the commander responded.

"We are not Mascien," Jev asserted, "nor are we a colony to the Masciens. We've severed our ties to the Mascien planet Amena when we settled this planet. Every person here is an innocent civilian. There is no military here. We're peaceful."

"They're still heading straight for us," one of Jev's guards said.

"Cycro," started a soldier, "you need to see this. There's something on its way here, and it's huge." Cycro gazed at the computer screen. He instantly knew what it was.

"Bring our fleet back and get the Kyriac's Knights back here as quickly as possible," commanded Cycro. "And, execute our evacuation plan."

"What is it?" the soldier asked.

"Fuses," he replied. Cycro picked up a communication device. "Dija," he started, "the Fuses are here. I need you to get back here now and find out from Marth how to defeat the Fuses."

"Cycro," Dija replied, "Marth is unconscious, and I thought we just killed the Fuses. How are they there?"

"Apparently, they don't have to travel as a single unit as we thought. If you can wake Marth up, do so. We need this. There are countless numbers of Fuses about to reach us. We'll get Dr. Land another time. Right now, we need to hold off on defense."

"I'll do what I can," assured Dija.

No longer talking to Dija, Cycro asked, "where is Xoz? Does anyone know?"

Karar was in a laboratory busily designing a weapon she thought would help combat the Fuses when she heard someone come in. It was very late at night where she was at on her planet, so she thought she'd be the only one awake. Since Earth and Kyriac were gone, she spent most of her nights working, trying to take her mind off of those painful memories.

After hearing the noise, she walked around a corner to where she could see the door, but no one was there. Being tired, she thought she may have imagined the sound, but the next sound she knew was real.

"Karar?" whispered a familiar voice. He wasn't in sight of her, but she knew it was Kyriac. She turned the corner again to see Kyriac standing there with only his face exposed from beneath his armor. His face was covered in ghastly scars the sight of which made Karar feel pain. "I shouldn't be seeing you, but I couldn't resist," he said.

"Oh my god," Karar gasped when she brought herself to say anything at all. Her hand covered her mouth to try to hide the shock and pain she felt seeing him again, and seeing him in this condition. "I," she started, but she couldn't finish. Starting again she said, "what, how?" She stopped herself and ran towards him with her arms ready and eager to wrap around him.

"Stop!" Kyriac commanded as he created an invisible barrier between them.

"Why? Kyriac, why?"

"I cannot touch you," he explained, "or you will die." He paused only for a second before continuing, "as I will soon die of this disease myself."

"I don't care," she cried.

"No, Karar. I do care. You see, I love you."

Her heart fluttered uncontrollably as she replied, "I love you too. That's why I can't stand to see you die again."

"I'm sorry I'm putting you through this again, but I had to see you one last time. I had to tell you how I feel." Karar couldn't take her eyes off of Kyriac for fear that he would disappear if she did. "I never got to tell you before how much I love you. I thought this would make things easier." Softly, he whispered, "goodbye Karar." He didn't want to leave her, but he knew he had to.

"No, stay," she demanded.

"There are billions of people in this universe that need my help. I have to save them all by stopping Dariah. I'm the only one who can."

"Quit being so selfless," she blurted out thinking more with her tears than her mind. She took a deep breath and continued, "why can't you think about what you want for once, or what I want?" Kyriac didn't respond, so she continued again, "stay with me tonight. Please, I need you here with me."

Before she finished her plea, Kyriac had gone, and with him, Karar's desire to do anything. Instead, she cried. She cried until the morning came, and tried to cry again, but with no tears left in her eyes, she cursed instead.

Chapter 28

"Am I dreaming? What am I seeing?" Ky couldn't make sense of any of the images he was seeing. Literally, millions of images were flying through his mind.

"Rise, Kyriac," commanded a deafening voice. "You cannot give up now."

"How?" Kyriac thought. *"Am I dead?"*

"Not anymore," the voice bombarded Kyriac.

"How?" Kyriac thought again

"I am Marsa," the voiced echoed. "Mother of Earth, Shaka, Ya and Ma. My child, Shaka, was among those that sacrificed themselves so that you may live once more, as a god."

"Am I still dreaming?" Kyriac thought.

"This is no dream. Now wake, for my children will guide you from here."

Kyriac did as he was commanded, gasping as life poured back into his body. His lungs filled with air as he stood up and opened his eyes to gaze upon the place where he had died for the first time with working eyes. *"I can see"* he thought.

"Yes," said a new voice from behind him. Kyriac turned around to see two people he recognized as Ya and Ma, and two people he did not recognize, but somehow he knew their names, Dija and Torscula.

"Come with us," Ya requested.

"Where?" Kyriac asked. "Why?" he added.

"To answer many of your questions," started Torscula. "I will tell you what has happened in the month you've been dead. Dariah disappeared from this universe until two days ago. None of us know how or why, but upon arriving back in our universe, he killed sixteen gods from this galaxy as well as conquering dozens of planets. In just two days, he has done all this. He now commands an army of over ten million soldiers of many different species who either joined him or are being forced somehow. None of the remaining gods are capable of stopping him. You, Kyriac, are our only hope to stop Dariah from his conquest."

"If he is this powerful, what can I do?"

"Every so often in an evolutionary process, a Mloris is born, a person with seemingly infinite potential. If this person were to realize their power early on, they could advance their species millions of years ahead in the overall evolutionary standings. In your case, an extreme set of circumstances forced you to exploit your power causing you to evolve further than normal. Only one other Mloris in the universe has done as much as you, Ricoba of the Mascien race. He advanced his race to where they are now, by his genetic code slowly spreading through his people. Because there was only one Mloris, each generation had to slowly breed into evolution. Ricoba is over a hundred times more powerful than any other Mascien. He, however, is far too old to be able to utilize his power. He has gained a vast knowledge of how the universe works, and we hope he'd be willing to share this knowledge with you."

"Then, is Dariah an Mloris too?" questioned Kyriac.

"Yes he is," responded Torscula. "but he is the only member of his species, so he cannot breed to continue his species."

"There's one other thing," started Ya. "This needs to be addressed as soon as we can, and that is that your muscles are decomposing."

"What?"

Ya continued, "Shaka's power was not great enough to bring you entirely back to life, so your muscle tissue dies rapidly leaving you with no strength. The problem is not as severe as is seems though, since there is a way to focus your internal energy towards the external muscle tissue in order to rejuvenate your cells. Basically, it leaves you tired, but you cannot age and you can quickly heal. We are sure that this will only slightly slow down your ability to gain power, but you mustn't over-burden yourself for fear of death. The four of us intend to stay near you to ensure you don't die while training."

"We also intend to get you into the battles to gain whatever knowledge we can about Dariah," added Torscula.

"For this, we have a plan," Ya continued.

"What we don't have a plan for is Dariah," Torscula pointed out. "And aside from you, we have no idea how he can be stopped."

"He expends a vast amount of power controlling his minions, so his power is growing far slower than it would otherwise; however, if he were to release all of his minions, he'd have a massive boost in his power, since he controls an estimated two million pawns. To be completely honest, we have no idea how much power he actually possesses."

"He has two million minions, tons of power, and what else?" insisted Kyriac finding the situation hopeless.

"Well, he has many, many other secrets and tricks that we hope to discover while we are preparing," Torscula responded, "but we can't be certain of anything."

"Don't forget the Fuses," Ya added.

"He wasn't controlling the Fuses," Kyriac asserted. "They were aiding him."

"Are you sure about this?" Torscula asked.

"Though blind, I could see him. He stood alone until Cycro's battle cruisers started approaching. That is when they swarmed around us, but they never interfered as though they wanted to see who would win."

"Or they wanted Dariah to kill you," Torscula suggested.

"No," Kyriac responded. "The Fuses are not with Dariah."

"Okay, we have two separate issues then," Ya concluded. "Kyriac, you will focus only on Dariah, and we'll be the ones to deal with the Fuses."

"We already have a plan to get us into Cycro's army, so let's go," Torscula stated.

"There's one thing I need to know," Kyriac started.

"Yes," Dija replied. "She is alive. You must understand that you cannot go to her."

"Why?" demanded Kyriac.

"It will only make your task harder," Torscula included.

"I don't understand what it could hurt," Kyriac pressed.

"Aside from our mission, you could hurt her," Torscula made clear. "What if you die again? She'd be torn apart. What if you touch her? She'd quickly die of muscular degeneration. If you get near her, you won't want to face Dariah; you can only cause this mission or Karar harm by seeing her, understand?"

Kyriac looked to the ground as despair drew over him.

"I know how you feel," Ya admitted. "And that's why you have to stay away from her."

"I know this doesn't help you any, except for some relief, but she loved you too," Dija explained.

"You're right," Kyriac choked out, "That doesn't help, and I'm going to see her. I just need a chance to explain everything. She'll understand."

"She..." Torscula was interrupted by Ya's hand on his shoulder.

"It'll only make things harder," Ya explained.

"I'm not going to die this time," Kyriac whispered. "She's all I've got."

"I finally understand you Kyriac," Ya admitted. "You didn't die for the people of Earth; you died for her didn't you? You're in love."

"What you're planning," Torscula was again interrupted by Ya.

"You cannot defeat him and save yourself at the same time. Especially not with muscular wear," Ya stated.

"Couldn't he," Torscula stated.

"Quiet," Ya commanded.

"Shouldn't we."

"Quiet I said."

"Why aren't we telling him?" Torscula demanded.

"Because deep inside, he already knows that there is really only one way he's going to defeat Dariah," Ya explained. "He'll be so weak that regardless who wins, he'll still die."

Chapter 29

"I think he found us!" a soldier, Pete, cried out with an escalating voice. "Dariah has abruptly changed course and is heading straight to us now!"

"It's no use. What can we do? What can I do now? It's no coincidence that all this is happening right now. Cycro, Jev and I are all under attack?" Karar was lost in thought. She was unable to get her visit from Kyriac last night out of her mind.

"Well?" asked a soldier near Karar.

Karar came back out of her own mind and responded in a solemn tone, "I don't know."

No one spoke for several painful seconds as they all waited for Karar to find a way to save them. They had always been scared, but not once had they seen her like this since settling on their own planet. That made them more frightened than ever before.

"I said I don't know," she shouted, frustrated.

"We have to do something," cried out another soldier.

"What does he have?" asked a voice from the doorway. Every soldier turned to see Kyriac at the door. If they weren't already speechless from fright, they were now.

Karar once again ran over to him, but this time, Kyriac created a wave of energy like the one Marth had created knocking Karar backwards onto her back. "Nobody touch me," he commanded. "What is he coming here with, and what do you already have set up defensively?" he asked again, more sternly.

"It's too early to tell right now for sure, but it's huge," responded Pete.

"Its size is the only reason we can track it so far out. He can't get here for several days if he traveled as fast as he could."

"Don't count on that," warned Kyriac. "He can get here whenever he wants. There's a reason he's going so slow. I'm going to go find out what that is. In the meantime, make this planet as defendable as possible." As soon as he finished speaking, his body dissolved into the air and disappeared.

"Was that?" asked Pete, stunned from everything that just happened.

"Yes," responded Karar. "He's back. He's going to fight Dariah again, but we're not going to let him die." Her voice built up in strength as she spoke. "Get every scientist and engineer working around the clock preparing weapons to fight Dariah and his armies, and make sure every soldier is equipped with the best weapons and armor. Get our spaceships all weaponized, and when all the soldiers are ready to fight, equip the civilians. If we don't all fight, we will surely all die."

"Karar?" questioned Pete.

"We're about to be the last humans in the Universe, and I don't want us to die right now," she barked back. "We have the capability of putting up one hell of a fight against him, so I say we do it."

"Half a million soldiers and six million civilians against an army of over two billion?" whimpered the soldier next to Pete. "What kind of odds are those?"

"They're good enough," assured Kyriac as he reappeared. "And, it's more like four billion at this point. He's coming with his entire planet. He has mobilized his planet."

"How?" demanded Karar.

"It'll be easy for him to support his army if he's got an entire planet in tow. Along with that, he has several hundred very large battleships, and for each of those, five or six smaller battleships. Each of these battleships is carrying a large amount of smaller, fighter-type, spaceships. His shields are impressive, and everyone and everything is equipped with our style of sola guns. Do we have anything better because those solas won't get through their shields anymore?"

"Yes," answered Karar. "We have much better solas now. Our personal shields are also vastly improved. On top of that, we have a shield extending into our upper atmosphere protecting the entire planet, and automated sentry batteries positioned just outside our upper atmosphere in orbit. As soon as anything gets in range, those will eliminate them."

"Just in case, can your shield stop a planet?"

Karar's mouth dropped open. "Would he?" she finally asked.

"Probably," answered Kyriac. "He's got many more, and he can easily raise a new army, but eliminating humans once and for all is an opportunity that won't come around again anytime soon."

"Get a team designing a way to make sure a planet cannot crush us," ordered Karar.

"While I was out," Kyriac spoke again, "I looked at Terra and Threna. Both look pretty ravaged. Sorry, but I think we're alone now."

"Then we should get working," Karar replied.

It was two grueling, sleepless days for the entire planet. Preparations were made in every possible way to ready the planet to engage the largest army the universe had ever seen.

"They're here!" cried out the sentry working in Karar's command post. "They're nearly within weapon's range."

"Get everyone who is assigned to flight to a spaceship. We won't engage them til we have to," instructed Karar. "When they're within range to fire upon us, get our shields up. How many batteries do we have in orbit?"

"One thousand six hundred and fifty-five," responded Pete, hesitantly.

"Let's hope they last," prayed Karar.

"Weapons away!" shouted the sentry.

"Shields up!" cried another.

A barrage of sola fire lit up the sky above Karar's planet as Dariah's weapons were repelled on the shield and the batteries returned fire. The entire hemisphere was lit up with no ability to tell if it was night or day. Soldiers' hearts sunk deep into the depths of their bodies knowing it was doubtful they would survive going up in that.

"Can we tell what's going on?" demanded Karar.

"No," responded the sentry. "We haven't lost a battery, but with all this fire, we can't tell if he's lost anything yet either."

"Is he still approaching?" Karar pressed.

"Yes, but much slower," the sentry replied. "Oh no," he quickly added. "The batteries are expending most of their ammunition to power their own shields. At this rate, they won't last long without getting resupplied."

"Easy fix," answered Kyriac walking into the room. "Quicken their orbit and have them get resupplied on the other side of the planet. Have our ships ready to bombard anyone who comes within sight. He's not as powerful cresting a planet. We'd have the upper hand back there, so it's a perfect time to reload."

"Do what he said," commanded Karar. "That means get all of our ships back there, as close to the planet as they can."

"Also, shrink your planetary shield to its shortest safe distance from the surface. This isn't going to be a short fight, so you need to conserve its energy," Kyriac directed. "I'll check in periodically."

"Where are you going?" questioned Karar.

"I'm going to see what I can do about shrinking Dariah's fleet."

"In space?"

"I'll be fine," he assured her. "There's a lot of strange things humans can do. If we survive, I'll try to teach you some of them so you can pass them on to future generations." With a wink, he disappeared again into the air.

"We lost a battery," announced the sentry only seconds after Kyriac had left. "And, another one. We're losing them fast!"

"He's not playing fair," stated a new person. Everyone looked to see Dariah standing among them. "You all know why I'm here, yet you continue to fight. In fact, you're fighting harder than ever. Already, several species have vowed to never fight again, but it seems humans and Masciens are relentlessly geared towards it." Everyone was frightened beyond words. "Oh don't worry; killing you like this wouldn't get the message across. I'll only do it that way if it comes to it. Right now, I just want to see how to get my army through your shield. It seems your shield takes energy from the planet. Well, the planet gets energy from your sun. We can take care of that. Thanks."

Right as he disappeared, Kyriac reappeared. Seeing the frightened faces, Kyriac had to ask, "What?"

"Dariah was in here," Karar finally responded.

"It's understandable he knows how to join matter too," Kyriac said to himself. "Why'd he leave?" he asked Karar. Karar explained what Dariah had said. When she was done, Kyriac continued, "his ships are probably big enough to eclipse the sun from us. Those big ones are a problem for me, but they can be done. If he gets them in place, I'll see what I can do. Right now, I'm moving your batteries inside of their ships. They're shields are worthless if the weapons are inside them. The batteries are then also a lot closer to Dariah's entire fleet that way too. I moved about twenty." Kyriac sat down.

Karar hadn't noticed him looking as tired as he was until now. "Are you alright?" she asked.

"I'm fine," he responded. "I just need a few minutes before I go out again."

"Karar," approached the sentry. "A few ships are moving away from the rest of Dariah's fleet. They might be on path to block out the sun."

"How long until they get there?" she inquired.

"Hours, maybe eight or nine," the sentry replied. "But that's a guess; I, I... I wouldn't know."

"The sun is slightly to the rear right now, so we've got to have our ships near the resupplying ready once they come into sight."

"I'll take care of them," assured Kyriac as he stood wearily to his feet.

"You need to take it easy," Karar insisted.

"I need to do whatever I can," Kyriac pushed.

"You said this fight was going to last a long time, what good are you if you're dead?"

"I said I'll be fine," he argued as he disappeared once more.

Frustrated, Karar began pacing and breathing heavily. "Have a few doctors in here for when he gets back," she ordered a nearby soldier.

For four hours, Kyriac came and went doing as much damage to Dariah's ships as he could before needing to return to regain his strength.

"It's not as easy as it would seem you know," he started speaking while lying on a cot in the command center. "Dissolving to energy, reintegrating in space, synthesizing oxygen out of rocks and metal, dissolving a satellite and reintegrating that within a spaceship. It sure does take a lot out of you."

Karar wasn't paying attention to Kyriac this time because the ships on their way to block the sun were about to crest the planet and be within sight of Karar's ships waiting on the other side of the planet. "As soon as they can see the ships, they should fire as hard and fast as they can," she ordered.

"Ah, ah, ah," stammered a soldier from across the room. "We've got incoming!"

"Who and where?" Karar call for.

"No readings, but it's moving fast and towards our planet," he answered. "No, wait, it's heading for those ships. It's going to collide with Dariah's ships." A few seconds later, he added, "it's an asteroid," in a puzzled tone. "How lucky is that?"

"It's not luck," Karar assured him. "It has to be Kyriac," she said, looking over to the cot.

"It wasn't me," Kyriac admitted. "There are no asteroids near here, and moving one big enough to do damage to those ships is impossible."

"We have an incoming transmission," announced the sentry near Karar.

"This is Dija of the Kyriac Knights. We thought you could use a hand," spoke the transmission. Kyriac abruptly sat up as he continued. "We're going to go ahead and embed this asteroid into those large battleships and then let us know where we are needed most." The transmission went silent, but the room filled with bustling whispers. With a smile on her face, Karar turned to Kyriac to see he was gone.

"Terra?" Kyriac asked now aboard Dija's ship.

"Mostly wiped out," Dija replied. "We got there after the Fuses. We were nearly too late, but Marth had come to and now we know how to defeat them. You basically just need to hit them with a hammer." Kyriac looked puzzled, so Dija continued, "we hit them with a strong shield. The shield won't give, so if it hits the Fuses hard enough, they get destroyed."

Responding to a huge explosion right next to their ship, Kyriac asked, "Are we right next to those battleships?"

"Had to make sure the asteroid hit," laughed Dija. Then, completely serious, he said, "You look exhausted. Show me your arms." Kyriac rolled up his sleeves to show arms that appeared to have had the flesh eaten away from them. "You're killing yourself. You can't keep this up or you'll die."

"It's under control," Kyriac challenged.

"No it isn't. You're doing this for her. Remember when we said that seeing her will make things harder? Well, you can't save her; you never could."

"I will save her," Kyriac promised.

"Oh yeah? I bet your feet are all about gone by now aren't they?" argued Dija. "How do your legs feel? How long until you can no longer walk?" Dija was shouting by this point. "We didn't bring you back so you could throw it all away. There's more than just her in this universe you know, and they're all counting on you here."

Kyriac didn't know what to say. He knew that Dija was right, but he couldn't let Karar go.

In a more peaceful tone, Dija continued, "everyone aboard this ship is willing to die for you as long as you're willing to live to save the universe from Dariah. We've got two hundred of the strongest demigods at your disposal. Don't you think you ought to go through with our plan?"

"Yes," was all Kyriac could say with his head hung low out of sorrow, knowing he couldn't save her.

"I brought you this," Dija spoke again, holding out Kyriac's sword. "Cycro had it."

"Thanks," acknowledged Kyriac.

"We have more incoming, this time behind Dariah's fleet," announced the sentry.

"Reinforcements?" Karar cried.

"No," responded the sentry. "This reads Mascien, and there are a whole lot of them. They'll catch up to Dariah within the hour!" The room once again cheered, but was cut off by Karar.

"Don't cheer yet," she growled. "Contact the Mascien fleet," she ordered.

"This is Karar of the human planet Armonia. I'm contacting you to propose a solution to your problem."

"What problem?" asked a Mascien commander.

"You'll never damage those ships. Your sola guns are no match for their shields. Our ships can destroy them. What our ships cannot destroy is that planet Dariah brought with. Can your ships destroy it?"

There was a thirty second pause before the Mascien responded, "yes, we can destroy it, but it'll take time."

"Meet my ships on the dark side of our planet. We'll have a better chance firing with our batteries opposed to against them."

It took three hours before the Mascien fleet could meet up with Karar's fleet, having had to go around Dariah's fleet to reach Armonia. As the combined fleet of humans and Masciens started moving towards Dariah, firing as they went, Dija's ship flew in front of them, trying to take a large portion of Dariah's attack.

"I think they forgot about us," Dija laughed to no one. His ship was the size of one of Dariah's smaller battleships, but his shields and weaponry were far superior.

As the two fleets got closer, millions of tiny spaceships poured out of Dariah's large ships, and thousands came from the Mascien ships. Together with the larger ships, they formed the most muddled mess of space combat there ever was. As they meshed, a flood of the same tiny ships came from Dariah's planet.

"I didn't forget," mocked Dariah as he appeared on Dija's ship. "You really are making things hard you know that?"

"Dariah," gasped Dija. Regaining his composure, he continued, "we're making things right again. That's what we're doing."

"I suppose you're to blame for bringing Kyriac back?"

"There were many gods involved in it, but I had my part."

"Gods? You're all so weak. In fact, I now know that you gods have gods. How strange that you could think you're all powerful when you worship something greater, and on top of that, most of you can die pretty easily by a mortal's weapons. That's not how I pictured a god. Did you know that there was a time on Earth when a group of humans worship certain animals? That's all you are, animals, and soon enough, people will realize that you're weak, and not gods at all." Dariah was enjoying his rant, but took a deep breath and redirected his speech. "To my point, even the gods intervening can't save these people. Look, my planet will soon crush that one." As he looked out the window, his planet began moving towards Armonia with obvious urgency. "All that firepower won't destroy my planet in time."

"Maybe I can," challenged Kyriac stepping up to where Dija stood.

"And, I thought you were hiding from me," Dariah revealed.

"I don't need to hide," Kyriac retorted. "I'll fight you now." Kyriac readied himself for Dariah's attack. With a nod from Dariah, they both dissolved into the air leaving Dija wondering where they went.

"The planet is coming at us!" cried out the sentry.

"I can see that," responded a frustrated Karar. To the Mascien commander, she continued, "concentrate fire. See if you can knock it off course."

"We're already trying that," the commander replied, equally as frustrated as Karar. "I've already lost half my fleet and we've barely scratched the planet, let alone the fleet around it. We're doomed if we keep this up!"

"I'll see what we can do," assured Dija. As he spoke, his ship broke away from the battle and headed to the planet. "Kyriac and Dariah are fighting now. I don't know where, but they were on my ship." His ship descended unaffected into the atmosphere of Dariah's planet.

Karar's heart sunk like the time he fought Dariah before. Old memories of pain stirred in her.

Once Dija's ship landed, the Kyriac Knights emerged and spread out with only a few left with the ship. Engaging every warrior they came across, they searched for whatever controlled the planet, or someone to tell them what controlled it.

It was Marth who found it. He came across a building, obviously using a massive amount of energy, which was guarded by at least fifty thousand soldiers. He walked through them, with his energy shielding them from getting near him as the other Kyriac Knights tried to fight their way to catch up with him. With ease, he made his way through the crowd and into the control room. Still surrounded by soldiers, he knew he couldn't affect the controls without dropping his energy barrier. Holding his breath as though it would save him, he drew his sword, dropped his barrier and swung as hard as he could at the control panel nearest him. With as much speed as he could, he brought his barrier back up. Nobody had gotten to him, but they were close. The control panel, however, was demolished. Unsure which panel needed to be destroyed to stop the planet's progress, he repeated this process twenty-four more times until he was too exhausted to continue. He hadn't fully recovered from the Fuses only days ago, so to have to do this again was taxing on his mind and body.

"Is the planet off course yet?" he asked through the radio.

"No," Karar responded on the other side. "You'll have to steer it now. Even if you shut it down, it has all the momentum it needs to collide with us. Find a steering column and pull towards the sun. Hopefully that, along with the Mascien firepower, will throw it just far enough off course." Karar had no perception of the peril that her request would put Marth in, but Marth knew he had to do it anyway. He knew which console was the steering one. It was the only one that looked like a cockpit. Once again, he drew his sword, only this time to protect himself. He made his way to the console, dropped his shield and began fighting those around him. They weren't tough for him, but there were a lot of them, and coming from every direction. With the hand that wasn't on his sword, he fondled the controls trying to make the planet turn. In mid-swing, he checked the screen to see if the planet moved. Over and over again, he took blows from swords and fists. The pain was intolerable, but he kept going. Finally, one of the soldiers broke through his armor cutting deeply into his leg. He cried out, but kept going.

"You got it!" cried out Karar a second too late. Marth's armor was broken through in his neck. Blood poured out from his lifeless body surrounded by dead and injured soldiers, but the planet was on course to miss. "Marth?" she asked. "Are you there?" As the Kyriac Knights listened on, they knew what had happened. They still were too far from the control room to help, so Dija ordered a retreat to the ship.

"They're correcting," announced the sentry. "They're turning back this way, but it might not be enough."

"Bring the shield in closer," commanded Karar.

"If it comes any closer..."

"Do it!" she shouted. The planet began to shake as tremors from crushed mountains and buildings along with the vibrations from the impacts against the shield from Dariah's fleet reverberated across the surface. Her breathing stopped as the two planets passed less than a hundred miles apart. The sheer noise of it was near deafening, even through the shield. The tremors collapsed every tall building that wasn't already destroyed by the shield. "Push the shield out as it passes!" she shouted, but no one could hear her. She pushed the soldier out of the way, and operated the shield herself. Pushing it way passed where it was before, it collided with the passing planet and gave it an additionally boost and it pressed against it.

"I found Kyriac and Dariah," shared one of the Kyriac Knights still on Dariah's planet. "They look nearly dead, both of them. I'm broadcasting." Everyone began to listen in.

"This war has to end Kyriac!" Dariah attempted to shout. "I'm saving lives. As long as this war continues, everyone will die. I see it. I see it in my dreams. I see it every night. I'm saving lives. Together! Together Kyriac, we're the only ones who can stop it. We are the strongest in the universe.

This much power between us, yet everyone else is fighting. We can put an end to it. We can show them that anyone who fights dies. They die as my brother did. Do you remember him? No one will fight if they feel what I had to feel when I lost him. This is the only way Kyriac. The only way. If you stop me here, everyone will die, and not just those you love. Everyone. Everyone will die. Masciens are waging war with everyone. We can stop that. People are fighting themselves. We can stop that too. This universe is massive, yet everyone seems to want to fight over it. There's no need to wage a war like that. This universe can be peaceful. I've seen it. I've seen planets where there is no crime. There is no murder or war. People don't fight. People don't kill each other. That's what I want. I'm not trying to ruin this universe. I'm not evil. I'm not what you think I am. We can be friends. We can be partners. We can save this universe together. It's all I've ever wanted to do, ever since I realized that killing can hurt people. For years, I've only gone after this one thing. People call me the devil. Did you know our gods wage war against each other? They convince us to wage war against each other because the more people they have worshiping them, the better they feel. On their plane of existence, that's food; it's praise. On our plane, it's death. It's murder. We can stop them. We have to. We're already gods. We're the most powerful gods. Why won't you help me? Stopping me won't stop this war. It will only escalate it."

"I told you there has to be another way," Kyriac responded, unbroken by Dariah's plea. "I promise you, I will find a way to bring peace that doesn't involve this much bloodshed. You're killing to prevent killing. Don't you understand how ridiculous that sounds?"

"If you could see what I do when I dream Kyriac."
"No," Kyriac interrupted. "You're delusional. You're insane. You're a hypocrite. Saying that you're killing all these people because if you don't, they might kill someone isn't how it works. Yes, people wage wars. People kill, but so do you. Recently, you're the cause of all the death. Can't you see that people who were once enemies have allied up against you? You've brought them together already. Now stop this killing. Dariah, I beg you, please stop this killing." Kyriac made it to his knees, and with his hands clasped in front of him, he continued. "You say you loved your brother very much, and he's the reason you're doing all of this? Well, there is someone I love on that planet you're trying to destroy. I love her very much, yet I can never be with her. Even so, I cannot bear the thought of her coming to harm. That's why I'm up here. I'm trying to save her, and you're the only one who can do that. You still outnumber us vastly beyond feasible

odds. There is no way we will win, even if you're killed. I'm supposed to disregard the fact that she'll die and come here and kill you, but I can't do that. I can't let her die. I know that you understand how I feel right now. If I could go back and stop myself from killing your brother, I would. I would take it back if it meant that Karar wouldn't have to die today." Tears filled Kyriac's eyes. "I... I'm sorry," he choked out. "I'm sorry I've made you become who you are now. I'm sorry the world didn't listen to you when you asked for peace. More importantly, I'm sorry I never loved you like the friend you tried to be."

Dariah had expected everything up to that point. He didn't know how to respond to Kyriac's gesture of friendship.

"Please Dariah, be a friend now, and save Karar. The universe has seen what war can do. Now bring it peace."

Dariah dissolved in front of Kyriac without so much as saying another word to him, but Kyriac didn't have the strength to follow him. His body was to the point that it could no longer be repaired. It was the most agonizing thing he had ever felt, dying in this way, but he held on. He wanted a sign that things were going to be okay.

"I don't have the energy to take your place," Dariah said when he returned a couple minutes later, "but I have enough energy to hold your head up and die with you."

Kyriac didn't hear anything after that, and it was only moments before his eyes and other senses failed too. He could only dream, and his dream went on forever.